SONS TO KEEP
A SISTER SEEKERS PREQUEL

BY
A.S. ETASKI

Published by Corpus Nexus Press
ISBN: 978-1-949552-24-9

etaski.com
miurag.etaski.com
www.patreon.com/etaski
linktr.ee/etaski

Cover Design by Eris Adderly
Book layout by DocKangey

It's been a decade since I began building the world of Miurag.

The beginning started in a small, dark place. Then it grew, season-by-season and become vast.

I recently published the seventh book of Sister Seekers, and the eighth book brings about one of the most significant events for this era. The Battle for Manalar.

By this point, the main story needed a prequel. Now, we have one.

Welcome to Miurag's underground city of Sivaraus, where our story begins.

CHAPTER 1

2883 S.E. – THE SANCTUARY OF SIVARAUS, IN THE DEEPEARTH

IRRWAER OPENED HER EYES WHEN THE MALE CHILD BEGAN COUGHING, WORKING TO breathe past his own spit. She neither lifted her head nor shifted on the cot until she was certain no others were in the small room. The stone door leading to the hall was closed, its ward spell in place; so was the innocuous, hidden panel on the far wall.

A whimper escaped the young Davrin. She smelled fear-soured sweat. The acolyte sat up on her cot, crossing her legs rather than touch her feet blindly to the floor.

"P-Priestess?" he asked in the dark. "I-is that you?"

Her lips twisted. *I've a long way to go, bua. In time.*

"Mother ..." he croaked, turning over. "Thirsty."

Would he expect that from her, were she here?

*Are any of these sons **not** spoiled?*

Irrwaer sighed, leaning over to inspect her slippers for dampness or pinching creatures. Once satisfied, she tucked her feet into them without lighting a candle. She waited.

"*Mother?!*" he shrieked, bolting upright.

Irrwaer jumped, clutching her heart where it tried to escape her chest. *Spinning goddess, child, shut up!*

"No," she answered gruffly as she stood up. "Acolyte Irrwaer."

He gulped, and she heard his heart race. He couldn't see her with or without light; his eyes had been bound with a blindfold.

"A-Acolyte. I am sorr —"

"I'll get water."

From her bed stand she poured two cups before moving to stand in front of him. Taking an audible slurp from the rim of her cup, she demanded, "Hold out your hands."

Irrwaer waited for him to obey before nudging the drink between his palms. The bua clutched it and drank swiftly, emptying it before she was finished with hers. She sighed again.

"Another?"

He flinched at the resentment leaking out. "Y-yes, please, Acolyte."

Irrwaer refilled his cup, still nursing hers as the child tried to consume this one more slowly. He would have to piss in half a mark regardless. She checked his bed pan, deciding to wait on it.

Five turns in the Sanctuary, invited to earn my worth, to wield the magic of a goddess, and I'm emptying waste pots for the Nobles' future breeding slaves. Pfeh.

She would rather be observing the ritual at the altar right now.

If Priestess Juliran weren't so protective of this pretty, delicate burden ...

"Why are you sick?" Irrwaer asked bluntly, sipping on her water with an arm crossed over her middle. "You were fine two cycles ago."

He turned his twice-empty cup in his hands. "I-I don't know, Acolyte."

"You weakened right before the ceremony," she said tersely, hostility rising. After all, *he* was the reason she was stuck here. "Your Priestess must focus on other duties with her First Son. If you aimed to distract her, to draw her pity in your jealousy —"

"I-I am not!" The bua shuddered at the mention of his half-brother. "Acolyte, I am sorry. I do not know why I'm sick."

She exhaled and took a nearby seat. For the cost Juliran had hinted she'd paid the Conceiver for this child, he possessed a disappointingly limp spirit, unrewarding to engage with for long.

Nonetheless, if he was awake, she must remain so as well.

At least he can't stare at me.

His coloring wasn't unusual at all: stark white hair, beautiful like a gossamer garden web; unmarked, dark skin; and scarlet red irises. His body was whole, symmetrical, and without defect; even his ears rose to perfect points without a hint of curl. Yet with that face alone, with those eyes, Irrwaer imagined every Matron and Daughter in Sivaraus would want to sample him once he was grown.

Assuming he doesn't insult someone and land on the altar, first.

"What is your name?" Irrwaer asked.

His lean shoulders lifted, his chin dipped, while his throat flexed in another swallow. "I am however you call me, Acolyte."

She scoffed. "What does your Priestess-Mother call you?"

The child hesitated. "Sil?"

"Sil? Are you not sure?"

"Th-that is what she calls me with others nearby."

"Fine. Sil." Irrwaer drummed her fingers, narrowing her eyes. "She has a private name for you?"

Mutely, he nodded. From the wince of pain on his lips, the acolyte wondered if Juliran's second son was magically compelled against speaking this name.

If so, is he like a Sathoet but pureblood? Hm. Is this common among the Conceiver's bred buas?

"Well," the acolyte continued, "does she ever —"

The ward of protection snapped from the door, and Irrwaer launched to her feet with a gasp, the pad of her thumb rubbing across the ring on her right hand as her first spell formed in her mind.

The stone door clunked against the bolt keeping it from sliding open.

"Irrwaer!" called Priestess Juliran through the molded stone. "Let me in."

Shit.

The acolyte hurried to obey, lifting the hand bar to its vertical position before pulling the embedded bolt out of its wall socket. Grasping the long door handle, she pulled the slab toward her to let her superior inside.

"Close and secure the door," Juliran said.

Exhaling in silent annoyance, the acolyte reversed her grip and pushed the handle to roll the door shut again, replacing its block-bolt before twisting the hand bar parallel to the floor again. She fervently wished they had materials lighter to work with. *Strange to have slow, heavy reinforcement for the sick beds, isn't it?*

The scent of fresh blood and recent magic struck her nose then, and Irrwaer turned around as Sil cried out in distress.

"Mother, you're bleeding! What happened?"

"Shh, quiet."

Irrwaer stared as the elder Priestess impatiently removed the bua's blindfold and held his cheeks between her hands, studying his face carefully without seeming entranced.

"How do you feel?" she asked. "Any better yet?"

"N-no," he answered, clutching his middle dramatically. "Where sh —"

"Shh, shh." Juliran pulled him against her, muffling his question to her breast as the Priestess stared vacantly at the smooth stone wall. Soon, her attention was distant, elsewhere long enough that Irrwaer lost count of her heartbeats in the dark.

No one else came to the door behind her, but she heard distant sounds of unrest in the temple. Her skin pebbled beneath the fine sleeves of her black and ivory robe. Irrwaer listened to the bua shudder and huff for breath against his Priestess's body, on the cusp of relenting to light a candle so she could mark the time.

Then, Juliran cut her head to the side, eyes fixed on the younger female. Although a Davrin Elf's dark sight lacked any color, the form and detail alone were enough for Irrwaer to know the Priestess had become aware.

"I need to speak with you," the elder said. "Wait for me in your quarters while I handle my son."

Irrwaer's stomach tightened on a frightened flip, but she masked it, bowing to her current tutor, her hands folded over each other. "Did anything go wrong with the ritual, Priestess?"

"Hold your words, acolyte. Wait for me, and speak to no one, understand? Make any excuse to keep your door closed and barred until second waking."

The young novice felt a shiver up her spine. "Yes, Priestess Juliran."

She turned around and left the infirmary, taking the hidden panel this time. Always much easier than using the door.

When Irrwaer arrived at the Sanctuary, she had been yet another Noble cousin to the Matron of the Sixth House. Though not ambitious enough to be the originator of most schemes, she'd had sisters and cousins aplenty to participate; to know the games and desires; when to observe and keep her mouth shut.

This upbringing had served her well moving into a large communal hall with other hopeful recruits for the Priesthood. She remembered it as a flood of abject misery after leaving her family behind.

The Priestesses of the Spider Queen were spoiled for choice among acolytes, with more "recruits" than they had need for. The Sanctuary was flush with messengers, scribes, assistants, free-flowing gossip, and hustling, young hands doing all menial tasks for the Daughters of Braqth.

The unremitting contests for the best space, attention, and desirable tasks contained a flux which mirrored water cycling through the pipes, but Irrwaer had learned enough tricks to earn her own tiny suite within the first three turns. For two of them, she'd been passed around to serve different Priestesses, seemingly on a whim, but always with the promise of learning pieces of magic as reward.

Though difficult to predict their moods at times, this was still better than the crush of plotting caits among rows of cots in the bunk hall.

I'll never live like that again. Those backstabbing, covetous slits might as well be a pile of demons chewing on each other's haunches.

Nonetheless, within her own quarters and with mage skills to better determine if anyone had entered while she was gone, Irrwaer had come to believe that someone was always watching.

Rarely were her modest belongings disturbed or missing, but sometimes she heard the barest scratch behind walls or above her head. Although no one had bothered to force her door while she was inside, there'd been other times an oppressive weight would flow in to sit on her while she rested in Reverie.

Occasionally, she awoke with a yelp or a garbled scream, unable to remember what she'd seen which made her fear imminent pain, death, or … something much worse.

The neophyte to the Priestesses of Braqth never truly felt alone in the Sanctuary.

Irrwaer. Let me in.

She looked to the barred entrance even as she heard the command spell in her ears. For an instant, the cait imagined refusing and staying on her bed. The next, she stood and opened the swinging door to her tiny quarters, allowing a Priestess inside for the first time.

What does she want?

How would her life change again once Juliran left?

The Priestess barred and warded the door herself while Irrwaer stood back. In truth, between the bed, the desk, and the changing closet, there was barely room enough to change places while brushing elbows, but the elder was neither concerned nor offended.

"Light a candle," her superior commanded.

Irrwaer obeyed, unsurprised she must use her own rations for this meeting. In the light, however, the acolyte noticed for the first time the fine creases at the corners of Juliran's eyes and the strands of gold shining at her temples. Irrwaer had estimated Juliran's age at four or five centuries, and yet she knew Priestesses who were older but not showing these same signs of maturity.

Why doesn't she try to hide them?

"Sit," commanded the Priestess, indicating the rough, fiberstalk mattress.

Irrwaer planted her bottom down, folding her hands in her lap and maintaining her posture. She stiffened when Juliran sat next to her. "I have a chair, if you wish, Pr —"

The Daughter of Braqth waved her hand impatiently, as though the acolyte disturbed her concentration, and the cait fell silent and waited.

Finally, Juliran spoke. "Sil tells me you protected him well. Served him water when he asked."

"As you bid me before you left, Priestess."

"Hm. And you did not touch him."

"Why would I?"

Juliran huffed, inspecting a sapphire ring on her finger. "Why the blind-fold?"

Irrwaer bit her lip. "I wanted to rest. His face is distracting."

Juliran smiled wistfully. "He *is* beautiful, is he not?"

The acolyte nodded mutely. "I feel no pull to him, Priestess."

The elder mother exhaled, her back straight. "I can tell. You seem to feel little attraction for anyone."

Irrwaer shrugged. "Anyone has an ugly side if you drop your guard. Attraction is just the gap under the door."

"Indeed." Juliran massaged her fingers like they were stiff, keeping her gaze on them and the fine chains connecting her rings to her wrist bracelets. "If not attraction, why is his face so distracting that you cannot sleep?"

Irrwaer maintained her guard. "Just what you said. He is beautiful but strange to most Davrin I've seen. Exotic, despite his normal coloring. I've never seen another bua who could be related."

Juliran's eyes were the same shade of scarlet as her son, and they slid toward her with skepticism. "Hm. Why do you seek to serve Braqth, child? Answer without the ritualistic platitudes if you please."

The novice chewed the inside of her cheek. "It seems I've been called."

"I said without platitudes."

"I mean *practically* called."

The Priestess arched her eyebrow. "I'm listening."

Irrwaer rubbed her palm along her thigh. "I ran into two Sathoet back on the plantation. They were … taunting me. Not a span later, my Matron sent me to the Palace to serve, offering no time after which I might return home. Reporting to the residence office, I was led to the Sanctuary. This seems obvious I was summoned, doesn't it?"

"Ah. You seek to serve because you have no choice."

Irrwaer smiled. "Better not to be deluded how far I can wander between the threads of the web, Priestess. This is challenging enough, and I have nothing else to do."

Juliran observed her. "Hm. Have you seen those two Sathoet again with their Priestesses?"

Irrwaer shook her head. "I don't know to whom they belonged."

"Would you recognize them if you did?"

"The demonbloods … all look the same to me."

Juliran huffed. "Not when you know from which wombs they emerged."

"I imagine time will correct my weakness, Priestess."

"Mind your tone."

"Apologies, elder."

The corners of Juliran's mouth twitched. "You're a dry one, Irrwaer."

"Thank you, Priestess."

Sil's Mother chuckled, some of her earlier strain having receded. "Do you know why you were assigned to serve me, after how many of us sampled you?"

Irrwaer kept back her thoughts on this. "I was not explicitly told, no."

"I've determined you have a stunted talent, hinted at in your aura and similar to mine and Sil's. This could be why he puts you off your ease."

Stunted?

The acolyte frowned. "Which talent?"

Juliran lifted her chin. "Healing."

Irrwaer laughed. Then bit her bitter tongue. "Apologies, Priestess."

"As you should be," she admonished. "Just because you've never explored your limits, don't mistake that some Priestesses can read you like a scroll misplaced by your own hand."

The acolyte felt her shield crack, and a deep chill leaked in. "I … I am sorry, Priestess. This topic has never come up before."

"You mean you never took effort to notice."

"Healing means touching other Davrin, Priestess. It's wise only to touch when necessary."

"You may believe that is the *sole* reason why I left you alone with my son during the ritual."

Juliran settled into a thoughtful silence while Irrwaer's fingers fidgeted with her blanket out of sight. She waited with lips pursed, mocking herself for laughing at her elder's evaluation.

Healing. Could that be? Why?

"Could you be satisfied working among the infirmaries as my assistant?" Juliran asked. "I can teach you."

Irrwaer's mouth tightened at one corner. "As your replacement?"

"Perhaps. It's too early to say if you can even access this talent, much less enhance it enough to be noticed by our Valsharess."

The younger massaged the back of her neck. The Priestess eyed her hand warily, and soon Irrwaer put it down again, laying both palms up to show they were empty. Juliran sighed.

"Does the lead healer over the infirmaries always become a Priestess?" Irrwaer asked, witnessing an inexplicable shine in the elder's eyes, even in the dark.

"If born a cait, yes," she said. "All healers are brought into the complex regardless of sex, however. You are correct that you were summoned. I do not know who already knows of your potential, but I have my guesses. I suggest you pay more attention to *who* is paying attention to *you*. Especially if you recognize the Sathoet who came to you."

Slowly, Irrwaer nodded her head, lacing her fingers together to keep them still. "I would like to serve you exclusively, Priestess. If you allow it, I'd rather not change mistresses again so soon."

"Done," Juliran said. "But work hard. And listen to what I tell you."

Relief.

Irrwaer nodded. "May I ask a question about the Sathoet?"

"Ask."

"Every Priestess has one?"

Juliran nodded. "She does."

"Only one? I mean, I've never heard of a Priestess with more."

The Priestess's lips spread in a sly smile. "Hm. Correct. Only one."

"Which means *I* must have one to become a Priestess."

"Correct. Conceiving and bearing the Sathoet Son is the final trial in becoming a Daughter of the Priesthood."

Irrwaer grimaced. "What happens after that?"

Juliran frowned. "After what?"

"After the birth." She waved a hand. "They aren't on the third floor with the rest of the Priestesses' children."

"Certainly not. The demonbloods would kill them if left unsupervised."

"Are they on another floor?"

13

"They are."

Irrwaer hesitated to ask which one. She'd never been above the sixth but heard there were twelve. "So, who raises them? The Priestesses, another group? How fast do they age?"

Juliran stiffened but then offered a smirk. "Perhaps you'll earn that knowledge later, acolyte."

"Understood, Priestess." Irrwaer leaned back a little, returning the space she'd thoughtlessly encroached upon. "Whether I become a Priestess or not, I would apply myself to that magic which you say I have."

"Do this," Juliran replied, "and your rise could happen quickly."

"Oh?"

"Yes, in two or three decades. It often does with healers. If you want a pureblood child of your own, however, bear them *before* that time."

Irrwaer wrinkled her nose a little. "Hm. I don't see where I would have time to be concerned for an infant."

Juliran shrugged. "Some acolytes give them back to their Matrons, but it's up to you."

"Why before the Sathoet? Could I not wait until after, like you did with Sil?"

The elder's smirk spread into a mordant smile as her fingers closed on her robe, bunching it until the creases shimmered. She hissed softly. "That's what I said when I was your age. I was too busy serving my superiors to catch my child, just like you."

The elder's bejeweled hand drew silk up toward her hip, showing first her ornate sandals and bare shin.

Irrwaer stiffened. "Uhm —"

"What they did *not* tell me," said her Priestess, "that I *shall* tell you, solely due to the rarity of your potential —"

The layers of Juliran's garment split as she brought the hem past her knees, and she reached with both hands to part the fabric and expose her thighs. She spread them wider.

Damn it. I thought she wasn't interested in caits!

"Listen to me!" Juliran barked as her acolyte jerked and covered one ear. "The demon son is, and always will be, the *last* child *any* Priestess bears from the strength of her own body."

The acolyte wrenched her eyes back up. "Wh-what?"

Juliran blew out the candle, plunging them into darkness.

"Look," she commanded.

With her eyes adapting and her Dark Sight emerging, Irrwaer stared at the Priestess's thighs. At the ugly, ragged scars.

Caused by claws and teeth.

The marks were old, and they glowed in Irrwaer's dark sight, somehow conveying color without any light. Subtly, swaths of crimson and indigo swirled, stitched together with harsh, black threads.

Spinning Goddess ...

"Did you hear me, acolyte?" Juliran sneered. "Or do you just want to plant your face there?"

Irrwaer ground her teeth, nodding her head. "I hear you, Priestess."

"Good. Keep listening."

Juliran kept her legs bare, opening them wider to show more scars. Some of her white mound fur was missing.

"Bearing the Sathoet *ruins* your womb. The scars inside and out cannot be healed, not by potion, magic, or time. This is how you are *ordained* in service to the Valsharess and Braqth for the rest of your life. This is how you obtain power beyond any House sorceress or wizard of the Tower.

"You must give *everything* to our queens, in this world and beyond. In return you receive the pinnacle gift: the bond-child with our goddess Herself, who allows divine power to flow through you. But there can be no more children after you've conceived and birthed the Grandson of Braqth. Those unwilling to give it all do not survive either the ritual or the birth."

Irrwaer swallowed, shaking as the markings held her captive. She stared at the ruined, dark flesh and scars which showed as purple Radiants.

Pain. I see only pain.

"Then how ..." Irrwaer asked hoarsely, "how did you have a second son? Sil. Is he pure?"

"He *is* pure." The Priestess pushed her robes down to cover herself again. "The Conceiver proved it to me."

"How did she obtain him? Is he your son in name only?"

Juliran's eyes widened in anger as she twisted her spine to lean into her acolyte's face. "He *is* my son! In all ways. *I* chose his sire. *I* gave him all I had. Sil *is* my blood, he has *my* magic!"

Irrwaer leaned back, her heart thumping. If so deliberate, why a bua? Why not a daughter?

"Th-then how?" the apprentice asked instead, waving her hand toward her lap and cursing the tremor that would not leave. "Y-you just told me the cost ..."

The Priestess's ire cooled as she reconsidered what to tell her. "Hm. Those are the Conceiver's secrets but understand that all Royal Consorts shall be blood-sons to the Priesthood. That is how we shall gift our goddess's power to the Nobility of Sivaraus, whose magic is weakening."

Irrwaer blinked. *It is? Since when?*

She sucked on her cheeks and stayed silent.

"You may not leave my service," Juliran reiterated. "If another Priestess requests you, I shall deny them. *You* will help protect my bua. You shall make certain no one abuses him when I am pulled away. In return, I will show you how to weave your magic and put it to good use, healer."

Hesitantly, Irrwaer nodded. She swallowed like Sil.

"I understand, Priestess. Thank you."

Chapter 2

2889 S.E. – The Sanctuary of Sivaraus

"You."

Irrwaer continued a few more steps. Just in case the Priestess spoke to someone else.

"Acolyte. Stop."

There wasn't another acolyte nearby. *Damned web.*

The apprentice paused and turned around. "Yes, Conceiver?"

The Priestess Wilsira Tachnathon stood just outside the ritual hall in a wrinkled, spider-silk robe of purple and black, smelling of sweat and blood. The powerful elder tilted her blonde-streaked head, her face still framed by an ornamental black headpiece. Irrwaer focused on the silver-web pendant resting in the hollow of her throat.

"Come," she beckoned. "We require more hands to clean the Assembly."

"Yes, Conceiver."

Irrwaer breathed out, a slow chill oozing down her spine as she followed the Conceiver into the one place she'd never been when the full Priestesses displayed their true power. She'd always been guarding one or more buas for Juliran.

Such opportunity had passed once again, with the crush of Davrin Nobles who had been here last eve gone back to the Palace or wherever they could rest in relative safety. The heatless torches were still lit, mostly red in color, and three other Priestesses were present, their servants and acolytes cleansing the polished stone under their supervision. The place still stank of fighting, magic, sex, and blood.

Irrwaer hesitated upon spotting three bodies lying upon the floor, those working giving them a wide berth. Two buas and one cait, nude and covered in fluids not far from the steps leading to the altar.

"Don't linger," Wilsira commanded, strolling directly toward them.

Hang my legs …

Irrwaer hurried to catch up, breathing shallow through her mouth to lessen the disconcerting odors filling her nose.

"You are Juliran's acolyte, correct?" asked the Conceiver like she already knew. "You work in the infirmary and help govern the children."

"Uh," Irrwaer cleared her throat. "I am, Conceiver. I-I do."

The Priestess lifted the hem of her robe and nudged the naked cait on the floor with the soft toe of her shoe. The youth didn't react. She wasn't breathing, either.

"Good. You will wash these three and wrap them for disposal. See that they are moved to the loading berth outside the kitchens. They shall be removed from the complex there."

She didn't share by whom. The cait swallowed. "What happened to them, Conceiver?"

"Braqth called for them, of course." The Conceiver narrowed dark maroon eyes. "I haven't seen you volunteer as tribute, have I?"

"Not since I arrived, Priestess."

"And when was that?"

Irrwaer bowed. "Not yet a decade. The infirmary and the third floor keep me very busy."

"So you haven't set foot in here at its most magnificent. Hmph. A decade, you say?"

"Almost."

"Well. If Juliran wove your education better, you could have seen for yourself what happened here."

"I confess my ignorance, Priestess."

"Have no worry, I shall speak with her about this." Casually, Wilsira pointed where the altar stairs formed a corner and continued around the platform. "Don't forget to burn their clothes."

Without awaiting a response, the Priestess left to direct someone else.

Thankful for an empty belly for once, Irrwaer got to work by bringing buckets of heated water and a stack of cloth from the kitchens just below. Washing corpses wasn't an unfamiliar task, but the acolyte had usually seen them suffering first, perhaps witnessed them slip away. They were usually still warm when she began. These three matched the slight chill of the stone beneath her knees; the grime leftover had had time to grow thick, flakey, or sticky.

Who were they? Are they all from the same House, or is more than one Matron to be informed of her children's divine sacrifice?

Irrwaer tamped down these thoughts, finished her work, and retrieved white sheets to wrap each body tightly. Then she plodded, panting, toward the stairs to collect the clothing. She reached for the soiled gown, shirts, waist-wraps, and sandals—

And stopped.

Tiny bumps erupted on her outstretched arm as the back of her neck prickled. Deep in shadow, one sleeve of the cait's gown was lifted off the stone as if held by an invisible hand. She heard something inhale as if drawing in the fading scent of the female Davrin. Irrwaer tugged once on the gown, and whatever clasped the sleeve tightened its grip.

She heard a growl.

Uh-oh.

Pupilless, yellow eyes appeared first, blinking at her while the rest of him gradually became visible in the crimson torchlight. As camouflage faded, he smiled, showing white fangs lining his leathery, black muzzle beneath his bat-like snout. The bushy, white mane flowed from the knobby apex of his skull all the way down his spine.

Sathoet.

A Priestess Son sired by the Abyss but, like the two from decades ago, Irrwaer didn't know whose.

The demonblood wore no clothes, was muscular and black all over but for his white mane and the coarse tufts at his elbows, knees, and crotch. If he stood up straight instead of squatting like he was, he would tower over any Priestess.

Was his Mother nearby? *She must be.*

No one else could control them if left alone to wander.

The half-blood chuffed through his nose and pulled on the gown, drawing her a step closer to him. The acolyte braced herself, and the soft, stained cloth pulled taut; neither hand let go.

Don't look away.

Someone always suffered when they did.

Irrwaer jerked once but failed to retrieve her objective. The Sathoet chuckled, showing her his pink tongue. It was long. The corners of his smirk turned up together at the same moment she noticed his swelling erection.

Chasing the tail of cold fear was a hot, welcome anger.

"Priestess?" Irrwaer called out, projecting her voice across the Assembly. "Your son is asking for you."

"Patience, Kerse," Wilsira answered near another Priestess. "We shall leave soon."

The Sathoet blinked in surprise then narrowed his gaze with a quiet hiss. "*Ssslit.*"

"Let go, bua," Irrwaer hissed back, jerking the fine cloth again.

It ripped on his claws as Kerse released it; the half-blood wrinkled his nose, apparently tired of the game. Still, he sucked in a deep pull of air through his nostrils, peering at her.

"*Affrraid,*" he whispered, his upper mane standing up.

The acolyte straightened up, pulling her shoulders back. "Of what? You?"

Without blinking, he cradled his partial erection in a rough, clawed hand. "*Thiss.*"

Irrwaer lifted her chin, resisted looking down. "I don't care. It's just a thing you have."

He chuckled. "*No sssire, no ssson. No Priestesss. Acolyte alwaysss a servant.*"

Irrwaer's annoyance and bravado faded in the wake of deep, intrusive fear. She bore restless Reveries in which her potential leveled off before she possessed any position of agency. The older and more familiar the servant in Sivaraus, the more creative their uses by their superiors whenever boredom struck.

The young have only so much time before they hit the stone ceiling.

The gossip about Wilsira and Kerse was impossible to miss; they were the only mother and son who entertained each other often with any cait of any status in the city. Now, Wilsira said she would speak with Juliran about Irrwaer's "education," while Kerse had just attempted a game with her.

Not good. Damn this web.

Ignoring the sibilant creature, Irrwaer gathered the clothing and left the Assembly to incinerate them. She'd come back for the bodies with additional help. And witnesses.

Juliran needs to know about this.

And, finally, Irrwaer admitted to herself that she needed to know more about pricks and pregnancy. Much to her consternation.

Better now before a more powerful Priestess chooses one for me.

"PUT THEM HERE," IRRWAER COMMANDED, WATCHING THE SIX KITCHEN SERVANTS labor to place three bodies on the berth. When they finished and looked at her, she said, "Now leave. Don't look back."

They obeyed without question, rushing back inside while Irrwaer remained where she stood, peering out the portcullis into the high-carved cavern through which the Palace-Sanctuary complex received its goods from the city. Often bustling with carts, drivers, and laborers, the Priestesses would close off the inspection gate, leaving merchants to wait in the chute and pause their deliveries prior to large rituals such as the one last eve.

Trade was still closed, and the dock sat eerie and quiet.

What do I do? Irrwaer touched the metal barrier, looking at the heavy mechanism to open it, estimating she could not handle it alone.

Wrap them for disposal. They will be removed from here.

Disposed where? By whom?

The answer came with the shush of many legs heralding shadow upon shadow. Where the Sathoet had made Irrwaer's skin crawl, the hint of one massive spider leg above her head — as long as she was tall — prompted a spurt of piss in her small clothes. Gnarled, black hands and tangled, white hair preceded a scarred Davrin torso. Following that, a swollen, arachnid abdomen moved on eight long legs, crawling with ease down the side of the Sanctuary. The acolyte backed away from the gate, quivering in dread.

Shit … What would have happened if she'd opened it?

The Driders would have gotten into the halls. If she didn't die by their hands, Irrwaer would no doubt be Wilsira's next "tribute" upon the altar. Unlike the Sathoet, who could be commanded by any Priestess, Irrwaer had heard only the Valsharess Herself could call off the Driders.

If *they* were here, then *She* was aware of how the ritual went, even if none had seen Her present.

Don't be stupid. Get away, now.

There were three of them, creeping mostly silent, sniffing and moaning softly in hunger. One of them squatted low, breasts on the stone, spider's legs bent up sharply as she reached an arm through the portcullis, scratching at the wrapping of the nearest corpse. Catching it, she pulled; the covered head clunked against the metal.

They won't fit.

Will they eat them through the bars? Pull them into pieces?

Idiot. Run …

Don't run! Walk. Walk away —

Irrwaer turned around and collided with a warm body. Strong, gloved hands caught her by the shoulders and kept her from stumbling back.

"Hey, there," a voice murmured, low and smoky. "Don't move."

Irrwaer recognized the style of red leather even without light showing its color; she stiffened, squeezing down on her overzealous bladder. For nearly ten turns, she'd avoided the Red Sisters in the halls of the complex. Now *this* following after the Conceiver? After Kerse? *After the creeping Driders?!*

This cycle would see her tripping face-down in front of the Valsharess next.

Two Davrin strode past Irrwaer gripped by the Red Sister. They approached the portcullis and the creatures now at the acolyte's back. One wore a fine quality cloak; the other wore mage's lightly shimmering robes. The acolyte was beyond shocked to hear a male speak.

"Are you sure, Lead?"

"You missed your chance to question this, Headmaster."

Headmaster?!

Irrwaer tried to look over her shoulder, but the Red Sister caught her jaw and forced her gaze to remain on her armored chest.

"Uh-uh, sweetmeat," she crooned. "Stay still."

The enforcer's chin grazed the top of Irrwaer's head, like a dare for some sudden move. Swallowing, the acolyte kept her eyes down and listened to the monsters at her back, the hissing, the rattling breath. Over that lay the beginnings of a chanting duet, and then Irrwaer *felt* the power of two casters launching a spell together. Her eyes pricked with surprised tears to sense their auras *merging*.

Effortless.

Exactly what Juliran struggled to teach her, with or without Sil to aid them. Irrwaer recognized her lack.

There's something between them.

Something ... open.

In the ensuing rush of magic, the Driders screamed, piercing Davrin ears in the partially enclosed docks. They were backing away from the gate.

"Be gone," said the mage Sister, her command tinged with quiet bitterness. "Let them be."

Irrwaer could not guess what the mages were doing with the bodies before the Red Sister hooked her chin and made her look up. She was showing her teeth, smiling down at the smaller cait with an expression as hungry for play as the Conceiver's Sathoet but lacked the devious sneer. Instead, Irrwaer imagined this Sister launching fearlessly into action at her elder's first order, accomplishing her task, and coming back to toss a celebratory slit into bed.

Irrwaer's quaking had lessened, fortunately, but only because the acolyte's body had begun to numb from her limbs inward. *Is that good or bad?*

"Protest, novice?" the tall fighter asked, holding her gaze with a smirk on her lips. Her head was covered by a custom-formed helm, and her hair must be close-cropped to fit that well.

Irrwaer blinked, willing to break eye contact first but unwilling to give the roughback an excuse to throw her around. *She could pick me up by my neck with one arm ...*

"No protest, Red Sister," she replied, her voice steady enough to impress herself.

The scent of worked leather and clean sweat strengthened as the warrior leaned down, moving her mouth close to Irrwaer's ear, and lowering her voice even more. "Won't your Priestess be disappointed? You let us interfere."

The acolyte shrugged off the blame. "She's not my Priestess."

"Oh?" The Red Sister breathed in near the skin of her neck. "Who *isn't* your Priestess, novice?"

Quivers returned as Irrwaer pursed her lips against remarks even more thoughtless. Which was worse: the Queen's enforcer touching and harassing her in a corner, or the Conceiver hearing later that Irrwaer had denied her power over her to the Sisterhood?

As much by habit as seeking a distraction, the acolyte glanced over the Red Sister's shoulder. *Someone's there.* Spying at the passage she'd exited with the bodies.

How ridiculous that the acolyte felt *relieved* when the Red Sister clasped both her wrists in one hand and turned halfway around. She called out, "You're made, Sancties. Come on out and join us."

Priestess Juliran glided out without hesitation, poised and elegant, holding her second son by the hand. She appeared annoyed and stern. "I've come for my assistant. Release her, Red Sister."

"Let her go, Jaunda," said the sorceress distractedly. "I don't need her."

"Yes, Lead."

With a disconcerting wink and a grin, Jaunda dropped Irrwaer's wrists, and the acolyte seized her opportunity, returning to her superior. Irrwaer reached for Sil's free hand as Juliran released his other and stepped in front as if to protect them both.

"Pretty bua," Jaunda commented, hands on her hips.

"Take your eyes from him, Sister."

The Red Sister defied the Priestess with a full-toothed smile and claimed another look at the shrinking youth before her gaze shifted one Davrin over, deliberately trailing up the Priestess's apprentice again, from her feet to her eyes. Seeing that desire again, Irrwaer quelled another shiver.

Shiiit.

Juliran narrowed her eyes and looked at the elder male inspecting the bodies from the ritual. He'd unwrapped the head of the corpse that the Drider had failed to pull through the portcullis. It was the cait, again.

"What are you doing out of your tower, Headmaster?" asked the Priestess, unusually haughty.

"Serving as I've been commanded, Priestess Juliran, I assure you."

"Were I you, Priestess," said the Lead, her gloved hand forming a fist in full view, "I would take what I was freely given and leave. You shouldn't be detained long from the fifth floor, agreed?"

Juliran bristled. "You overstep your power if you think that would work out for you, Varessa D'Shea."

Jaunda cleared her throat. "I'm sure the acolyte knows more about these bodies, Lead. She's probably more useful, anyway."

Irrwaer had *never* heard her Priestess growl in her throat like that before; Sil heard it, too, and leaned closer, squeezing her hand. Then, Lead D'Shea stood straight and looked at them fully for the first time, her cunning gaze taking all of them in. Helplessly, Irrwaer glanced at Juliran, squeezing Sil's hand back such that he grasped her with his other.

Too hard.

"If you wish to interrogate my acolyte, Lead D'Shea," said Juliran dismissively, turning and motioning for her son and apprentice to move toward the passage, "you will do so under my observation. You may find her in the infirmary at your convenience." She stepped once, paused, then smiled over her shoulder. "I will even provide you a room."

The way D'Shea squinted at the Priestess suggested a personal jab. Irrwaer kept her face placid as always, however, despite this persistent urge to pass her water with every successive threat to rear its head.

She'd slipped disconcertingly close to the center web this cycle.

This is a sign. Or a warning.

Did she have it in her to become a Priestess, or would she be a servant until she died?

Juliran had better not be lying. She must have more to teach me than this.

"Well, you stepped knee-deep into the muck this time."

"What would you have me do, Priestess?" the cait retorted in frightened frustration. "Snub the Conceiver and shirk her orders?"

Juliran exhaled as her pacing slowed. "No. You acted correctly for the circumstances, and I will obtain a meeting with her before she summons either of us. Although, you could have left with the servants at the dock. That might have spared you the attention of the Driders and the Sisterhood, if not Wilsira and her son. You're known to the Headmaster as well and will be mentioned to the Valsharess in his report."

Irrwaer bit her lip, a chill encasing her stomach. *What is happening here?* She straightened her back, gathering ambition which had been glowing like a steady candle for decades now without causing a flare.

"There's no undoing it, I know," she began. "And you've tutored me only gradually while Sil grows —"

"I've given you a *realistic* foundation," Juliran snapped. "Something rarely gifted among acolytes."

"Yes, my Priestess, I'm grateful. Do you want me to remain in the infirmary *and* become a Priestess as well?"

"There are no other possible healers," came a tired, bitter reply.

Close enough.

"Then if I must guard myself as much as the buas from now on, my Priestess, how do you recommend approaching this challenge?"

Her elder was soothed enough to give this concentrated thought, earning another silent prayer from Irrwaer for her chance in serving *this* Priestess. A grounded, competent matron who had more in common with Irrwaer's upbringing than any Davrin she'd met.

"It would not surprise me," the Priestess considered, "if D'Shea is preparing another obstruction for the Conceiver using that cait's death off the altar. You, my apprentice, are caught as the witness to the doings of both. Tell me, is there one you'd curry more favor with? And if so, why?"

Irrwaer made a face. "It seems obvious I should curry favor with the Conceiver."

Juliran smirked, arching her brow. "Is it obvious? Again, why?"

What?

Her certainty faltering, the acolyte chuckled nervously. "The Priesthood and the Sisterhood oppose each other at every turn, fighting for the greater influence in the Palace with the Queen. The Red Sisters wouldn't listen to *me*, they have no use for me, the Lead even said so. And Wilsira would make us suffer for undermining her around her rivals."

"Hm. True. Yet you know many others do *exactly* this because they want Wilsira's influence, and the Conceiver expects it. She enjoys honing her wit against them." Juliran paused. "So, you'd curry favor with a Priestess because … she's a Priestess, and we're choosing sides based on this identity?"

Irrwaer made another face, crossing her arms as she gazed into a dark corner of her Priestess's chambers. "Sounds too simple, hm?"

"Well, the simple *are* easiest to control. I've never seen you as such, Irrwaer. You notice the gaps, and sometimes you hide in them. What else do you see around Wilsira and D'Shea?"

"Kerse," the acolyte answered with a shudder. "He wants to play with someone new, and he knows I'm … unfamiliar with males."

Or with anyone. By choice.

Juliran nodded. "Agreed, and this shall come up again, if only because the Conceiver enjoys commanding nervous caits to submit to her half-blood son. I think she enjoys caits enduring him as they choke on their disgust."

Irrwaer gulped down nausea. She may be one of those. She'd been lucky thus far staying out of others' beds, but that streak of subtle fortune had dissolved like Kerse's camouflage at the altar stairs, leaving her inexperience and fear exposed.

If she were called to the Conceiver's chambers, the acolyte knew she must obey and spread but would feel nothing. At first. Then they would laugh at her and no doubt escalate their antics to get a more entertaining reaction.

If not pleasure, it must be pain …

Everyone in Sivaraus must be rutted sooner or later.

"What else, apprentice?"

Irrwaer gladly blinked the horror away. "Hm? Oh! Ah ..."

What else? Or who?

"The ... Headmaster," she answered, "with the Lead Sister."

Juliran hummed. "What about them?"

"They merged auras, like you've tried to teach me, like I've heard of battlemages. Enough combined willpower to scare off the Driders."

"Mm. That's impressive. I wonder if the Valsharess knows?"

Irrwaer made a mental note but wasn't finished. "They were also like you with Sil when he boosts your healing."

Something about the observation that made Juliran stiffen. "Oh? Is it different from me and my Sathoet at the altar?"

"I believe so."

"How?"

Irrwaer bowed before providing the recitation. "Only one Priestess can guide an Abyssal ritual, or we may lose control of it. The strongest will dominates the rest, including the Priestesses and their Sons, drawing from them. It is one of the quickest but most risky ways to raise one's rank if a rising Priestess can wrest control of an elder's ritual and lead it to success."

"Mm. That's correct, but you haven't answered the question. How is this unlike Sil and me? Or D'Shea and the Headmaster?"

The apprentice waved her hand. "It just feels *different*. The other mage is pureblood, male but *cooperative*. He is lacking the impulse the demonbloods are born with, to disrupt our order or exploit weakness or distraction. It may not match the power of the Sathoet but it's more reliable. I only did not have a good example besides you and Sil until now."

"Ah." Juliran's wary eyes brightened somewhat. "Well done. Many are double your age and never see this. Try to remember this and keep an eye on the pureblood buas behind the more powerful elders. It may serve you well." She sighed. "What else, my acolyte?"

"What else?"

"There is more to Sivaraus than caits and matas with cooperative buas, is there not?"

The apprentice frowned as the final, powerful memory on the dock returned. "The Red Sister. Um, Jaunda."

"Mm-hm. What about her?"

"She was ... sniffing me." Irrwaer rubbed her arm. "Like Kerse was."

Her Priestess looked oddly pleased. "Indeed. The Red Sisters are similar to Kerse in that way. In case you were unaware."

Similar?

"How? She's not the Lead's daughter, and she's not a bua ..." Irrwaer touched her lips to stop herself. "Wait, the ... um, attachment?"

Juliran chuckled, nodding. "And spreading intimidation on behalf of her leaders. In their barracks, the wielder of that false cock is on top, not serving beneath as we'd expect. Perverted, subversive cunts, the lot of them."

Irrwaer blinked. *The wielder of a false cock ... ?*

"Such behavior unsettles the Matron Houses to their core," Juliran continued, wryly amused, "and helps keep them in line. The Valsharess has supported how the Prime keeps city order for centuries."

The acolyte stood in quiet thought, trying to blend the unlikely occurrences of both a Sathoet and Red Sister implying they wanted to mount her within marks of each other. Neither would be serving underneath her if they did.

Hm. If I were to open thighs for one, which would I prefer? Who might teach me more?

The cait guessed her answer from how different the nervous sensations felt in her gut.

"Something else I will tell you," Juliran said, breaking into the unfamiliar scenarios in her head. "A crucial factor in this snarled web is yet to be sorted out."

The acolyte focused, studying her Priestess's cunning countenance. "What factor, Priestess?"

"Before I answer, you must understand that knowing could aid you in gaining the future you want, but only if you do *not* breathe a word too soon and lose your advantage."

She nodded. "No breathing, Priestess. Just listening."

Satisfied, Juliran touched her abdomen, waiting until her apprentice's eyes followed before delicately hand-signing the revelation.

★The Lead sorceress is pregnant. She will come to us, to our floor, when she can no longer hide it from her Prime. This is inevitable.★

Irrwaer stared, pondering their cyclic duties upon the fifth and third floors. Feeding, cleaning, tending. Illness, poisoning, injury.

Death ...

And birth.

I will even provide you a room.

Juliran's remark made perfect sense now, and it struck home that there truly *was* a choice for Irrwaer in this tangled mess. Who *would* she curry favor with now that she was noticed? *And why?*

The acolyte knew the answers to these questions. She wanted to learn how to blend her potential with another before participating in her first ritual. She wanted confidence like the sorceress. She wanted to get around this magical block and understand how to adapt when her time came.

Irrwaer also *needed* practical experience in coupling and cock-handling, whether she craved it or not. She could shrink from it no longer. She had no chance to survive a summoning, a demon, or his offspring without it, but she hadn't known where to begin that wouldn't see her controlled by a more powerful female.

What if the one to teach her to handle a cock *was* female? What if she slept somewhere outside the Sanctuary and had other games to play in the city after she was sated? A Red Sister might dominate her body as she pleased but lack the access and interest required to twist Irrwaer's will against itself in games such as the Conceiver was known for.

Yes.

Time to learn new skills, or Irrwaer wouldn't recognize herself in the next decade. Juliran had been trying to teach her but without progress where it mattered. Looking back, the Priestess seemed too concerned with Sil and placating Wilsira, in paying whatever costs and agreements still tugged at her robes. Irrwaer had been recruited to keep the infirmary and nursery running in her absence.

At the same time, the elder Sanctuary healer could not be less subtle about suggesting that her acolyte not take the same path to power she did. Not when this surprise stumble into politics had opened more options than she'd had a cycle ago.

Jaunda or Kerse? D'Shea or Wilsira?

The acolyte was a toy regardless; Irrwaer knew and accepted this. But what if she was also a useful tool, self-shaped for the inevitable choice, because Juliran had given a big secret?

Lead D'Shea is pregnant.

This left the question of whether the Red Sisters would arrive in time to interrogate Irrwaer in the infirmary before their Lead sorceress was placed in residence to complete her pregnancy. The way they spoke to each other, Irrwaer thought it a good chance that Jaunda would be sent to check in now and then.

I can work with either outcome.

Irrwaer smiled as desires bolder than she'd ever had quickened in her belly. A peculiar readiness settled in her mind like a gossamer shawl, carrying upon its fringe the options to choose from in what came next.

Juliran recognized the look, smiling back before turning to check on her pureblood son waiting obediently in the washing room.

"Make your rounds," she instructed, "and I shall return shortly and teach you how to prepare."

CHAPTER 3

A SEMBLANCE OF ROUTINE RETURNED OVER THE NEXT FOUR SPANS, WHETHER THE underlying anticipation belonged to Irrwaer and Juliran alone or it somehow spread to others. Her wait for the Red Sisters to show up on the fifth floor of the Sanctuary crowded the same space of concern as the Conceiver calling on Juliran about Irrwaer's lack of education.

One eve, after the acolyte had tended a rush of fight-related injuries on the third floor, her Priestess finally had some good news.

★Wilsira has forgotten about you for the moment,★ Juliran signed. ★Even if Kerse hinted he wanted to play, something else occupies her thoughts now.★

Irrwaer's shoulders relaxed, her chin dipping. ★Same with the Red Sisters? If they had needed my witness, it seems they'd have come by now.★

With a thoughtful nod, Juliran shrugged. ★D'Shea and Wilsira are posturing over that cait's corpse from the ritual. You are still in the middle. Do not let down your guard yet.★

★Do you know who she was?★

Juliran nodded solemnly. ★A young cousin of Matron Byu'Fel.★

Irrwaer's mouth opened. ★Our High Priestess's family? The Conceiver had me try to feed a daughter of the *First* House to the Driders?!★

The Priestess smiled grimly. ★Indeed, if Lead D'Shea and the Headmaster hadn't stepped in then, I believe Wilsira would have blamed you for the 'mistake' in clean-up and had you suffer the punishment by the Matron.★

The acolyte's core froze, her fingers going numb as she gritted her teeth and tried to sign. ★She ... she *told* me to.★

★I know. Convenient fodder between the Houses Byu'Fel and Tachna, even reaching into the Sanctuary.★

With a low growl, Irrwaer ceased wallowing in her shock. *Of course. A near miss, that's all.* An impulse as natural to the Conceiver as swatting a racha crawling out into the open.

★Do not show your resentment to anyone,★ Juliran counseled. ★Do not tell anyone but also do not forget. Pay attention to who speaks to you, discover what they want. Tell me everything. I don't want to lose you, Irrwaer, you can survive this. I would see you ascend to a Priestess, because Braqth and the Valsharess cannot waste our healers.★

Irrwaer swallowed. ★Yes, my Priestess.★

Only one cycle later, she was tested on this very advice, navigating one of these encounters like stepping barefoot among poison-tipped caltrops scattered on the floor.

Irrwaer paused in her work and bowed to the youngest Priestess in the Sanctuary. "Lelinahdara. Goddess Rise."

"Acolyte," Tarra acknowledged with a bright-eyed smirk, her eyes open wider than necessary, for she knew well how discomforting their strange green color was beneath heatless candlelight.

Like glimpses into some elsewhere far away ...

Tarra strolled around the room as if inspecting its cots and supplies, noting the setup and current three silent, adult patients pretending to sleep. Irrwaer caught her glancing at the wall hiding the secret entry, casing the space.

"How may I serve you, Priestess?" the healer's apprentice asked forthrightly.

Two sharp emeralds peered directly at her, and Irrwaer's eyes landed on the floor as her better closed the distance with the grace and certainty of a spider approaching its next meal. The apprentice kept her poise, squaring her shoulders as she thought of the scars hidden between the Priestess's legs. They would be much fresher than Juliran's; Tarra's Sathoet Son was still young enough to be kept away from his "brothers" on the twelfth floor.

No one escapes these marks if they prove worthy.

I'm curious, Irrwaer, Tarra signed privately, her hands hidden from the patients. *How would your Priestess secure a patient of greater importance than these.*

She waved her hand at the two servants and minor Noble brought over from the Palace.

Irrwaer signed in kind. *We have smaller rooms with protective reinforcements, Lelinahdara.*

May I see one?

As with Wilsira, there was not a way Irrwaer could deny her without immediate consequence. Once the acolyte had secured her patients, she guided the Priestess from one drab-stone room to another down the hall and around the first corner.

"Why does Juliran not decorate this level more?" Tarra asked, seeming bored with the clean, spacious passage.

"It helps cut down on hallucinations," Irrwaer answered.

"You jest me."

"No, Priestess. Many patients who arrive are intoxicated, poisoned, or have inhaled too much incense. Sometimes we use more of the same to dull the pain of the injured. My Priestess has shared many stories with me of Davrin attacking the paint on the wall or using statues or hanging art as impromptu weapons."

"So, they can't be trusted for their own safety? Hmph. So be it."

Irrwaer broke the ward on an empty, secure cell, and turned four different latches to slide the heavy door aside. Tarra entered first, supremely confident Irrwaer would not succumb to the impulse to lock her in. Instead, the acolyte slipped her hands into her robe and rubbed the "panic ring" on her finger.

"Inside," Tarra commanded as if she'd sensed something. "Close the door behind you."

Irrwaer sighed inwardly and obeyed. *Juliran will be here soon.*

With only a cot and a washstand to avoid, Tarra ran her hands along the walls as if searching for another way out of a private chamber little larger than Irrwaer's personal one. The young Priestess began with a knowing remark.

"Runes to dampen sound traveling to the hallway but not this wall here. Interesting. You have ways of moving between these rooms, unseen by casual servants, correct?"

Irrwaer smiled a little. "Every Priestess does in her area of specialty."

"Mm, you would know better than most." Her eyes were not as unsettling in the dark when she turned her way. "Do you enjoy the infirmary over other areas since you arrived?"

Irrwaer bowed slightly. "Priestess Juliran was right about my potential."

Tarra arched her brow. "So, you can heal with your hands?"

"With proper preparation, yes, though her magic is still stronger."

"*Pfeh.* You haven't pushed yourself."

Irrwaer fell silent as Tarra walked the perimeter of the care room a second time, running her fingertips lightly along the walls. She wore similar rings, bracelets, and fine, interconnected chains like Juliran.

"What of birthing?"

"I have experience, Priestess."

"Your own?"

"No, Priestess."

"Hm."

Tarra fell still for a moment, her eyes vacant and an odd shade of grey in the pitch black. Then she blinked and shook her head once, making a poor attempt to sound blithe. "What about the Red Sisters? Have you ever tended one of them?"

Irrwaer's middle tightened. "No, I believe they have their own infirmary in the Cloister."

The youngest Priestess smiled at her. "For most things, they do. What about ensuring one gives birth to a safe and healthy child? You understand the risks they must take with their bodies to perform their role. The Cloister is no place for an expectant mata."

The acolyte frowned in thought then lifted her eyebrows. "Oh. I would help assure this, of course."

"What if she tried to leave when the Queen's Law bids that she remains here until birth? What if we would all suffer if she got away from us?"

"We have sedatives unlikely to harm the unborn," Irrwaer answered. "And restraints if she harms herself."

Smiling now, Tarra looked around at the solid room with a high ceiling.

"A secure cell, it seems. Excellent. I admit I've been so busy on other floors I hadn't thought to become more familiar here until now."

Until now. Damn.

Irrwaer squinted. "Forgive me for asking, Priestess, but who are we expecting — ?"

"Shh," the Priestess cooed, placing a finger to her lips with a wink. "I have another question, Irrwaer."

Sigh.

A voice boomed, and both caits' feet left the smooth stone.

"Hey! Open up, this room's taken!"

"Corpora! Not amusing!"

"Sorry, Lead."

Irrwaer's mouth sagged as she recognized the Lead sorceress and her muscular guard.

"How are sounds getting through!" Tarra hissed at her other side.

"The runes block from within only," the acolyte said, spreading her hands. "It's louder from without as a result."

"What incompetent wizard *made* these runes?"

"Irrwaer, are you in there?" Juliran called clearly. "Open the door."

Her middle jumbled, her thoughts flying in all directions, Irrwaer moved to obey her superior over her interrogator's look of displeasure, but Tarra seized her arm, squeezing hard enough to leave nail marks through her robes.

"Don't you dare," Tarra growled. "You'll let me out the secret passage first!"

"With that delay," Irrwaer replied, "Juliran and D'Shea will know I wasn't in here alone."

"Of course, but you'll not tell her who."

Perhaps unwisely, Irrwaer scoffed. "They both outrank you, Lelinahdara. Even if I resist, they can force me."

How about you introduce yourself and try for advantage instead of fleeing, you conniving slit?

The acolyte bit her cheek, pausing only until Tarra's grip loosened enough for her to pull free and continue to the door. It always took longer to open the door from the inside, requiring a sequence of touch-runes and a specific bolt from her pocket added to the mechanism.

Irrwaer hurried, caught in a poor position once again and ill-equipped to meet Lead D'Shea and her security Corpora. The moment the door rolled aside, the acolyte gulped and turned to stand at attention, even less prepared for the High Priestess Roshen Byu'Fel standing behind them.

Fucking Void!

The bored elite raised an eyebrow at Tarra, ignoring Juliran's apprentice. "Lelinahdara? Where is your son?"

The youngest mother bowed. "He's secure, High Priestess."

"But not where the rest of them are, correct?"

"For certain not, Your Sanctity. He is still too young."

"Then you shouldn't leave him so soon."

"I requested her assistance, High Priestess," said Juliran with a calm and respectful nod that tested the caits' composure. "We appreciate the second look at the runes, Lelinahdara, given the illustrious status of our new patient."

"Ah!" Tarra bowed to the elder Priestess. "Of course, Priestess Juliran. Summon me anytime."

D'Shea narrowed her eyes; she wasn't swallowing this lie, but Roshen seemed to for now. "I see. Well, it seems crowded in here. Perhaps Sister Jaunda can escort the acolyte and novice confessor back to their duties then see herself out?"

"No!" barked the sorceress. "I would speak to my Corpora before she returns to give her report to Elder Rausery."

"I can come back, Lead." Jaunda looked at Juliran. "Right, healer?"

She smiled. "Of course, you may."

"Then so be it," High Priestess Roshen said shortly, flipping her hand. "Be gone, young ones. I have elsewhere to be after this."

Juliran tilted her head. "Your presence enhances our oath to any Red Sister who needs sanctuary for her child."

The enmity and contempt in the Lead Sister's eyes could not be clearer. For an instant Irrwaer wondered if they were all about to be engulfed in flames, but then D'Shea took a deep breath, released it, and stepped inside of her own volition.

Nudging past Irrwaer, who flattened herself against the wall to make room, the pregnant Red Sister sat on the cot and leaned back on her cloak, crossing one leg over another. Her belly just pressed out against a red leather more supple than Jaunda was wearing.

"Very good." Roshen motioned them out.

Tarra and Irrwaer moved to join Jaunda as Juliran led the High Priestess inside. Then the door shut again without another word. Nothing could be heard inside, but the small hairs on their napes informed them of the ward being put into place.

Irrwaer jumped when a hand clapped atop her shoulder.

"A bit tense, sweetmeat," the Corpora observed. "What were you both doing in there?"

"Inspection," Tarra said tartly, striding back toward the patients Irrwaer had left behind. "Now we're finished, let's not disturb them further. I have a son to return to."

Jaunda caught Irrwaer's gaze, who stared at her, eyes wide when she'd almost rolled them.

Smirking, the Red Sister signed, *Guessing not quite?*

Irrwaer bit her lip, and the grinning enforcer slapped her on her back.

Ow!

Her jaw tight, the acolyte stood in place, unsure how to respond to that strike.

"Well? Come on. Let's go back."

Go back? Alright …

The Priestess's apprentice got her legs moving as she accepted that a Red Sister would be wandering around the fifth floor until her Lead called her to "talk" one more time.

Assuming I can keep her here on the fifth.

Irrwaer wasn't eager to be blamed for whatever trouble this one could find elsewhere in the secretive complex, and this seemed like her best opportunity to learn about rutting.

If she could gather the nerve to ask her about that "attachment."

I'll figure it out.

CORPORA JAUNDA LEANED AGAINST THE WALL BESIDE THE OPEN DOOR AS IRRWAER took the vitals of each patient, each again pretending to sleep. Against expectations, the Red Sister touched nothing and made no snide remarks as the healer silently emptied bed pans, salved then rewrapped wounds, and provided more food and water for when they dared to open their eyes.

They're getting better without too much magic, at least.

They could return to the Palace soon.

"Come," Irrwaer said, lifting her basket of soiled supplies with as much confidence as she could manage. "Let me secure them."

The Red Sister grinned, pushing back from the wall. "Where we going?"

"Drop this off to be cleaned. Then, um, take inventory."

"Then, um, hmm?" the fighter crooned. "Fun."

"Hardly."

Irrwaer had spiders skittering in her belly, and Jaunda said nothing through the many steps of locking her patients in, depositing their filth, and tracking down the next warded closet which needed to be checked for signs of theft and be restocked. Only once Irrwaer had dispelled the protection and opened the door did the Red Sister speak.

"You always work this hard?"

The acolyte made a face over her shoulder. "Hm? What else would I do?"

The Corpora shrugged. "Maybe you're scared. Trying to hide it."

"*Pfft,*" Irrwaer scoffed without thinking. "I've always been like this. Being lazy or incompetent is the fast way to the worst work. I prefer to be busy and have a comfortable place to sleep when I'm finished."

"Yeah?" The Red Sister sounded pleased. "Simple pleasures earned for obeying your elders, eh? Me, too."

Irrwaer paused, reflecting on her words. *Does she ... is that suggestive? Does she think I was being — ?*

Jaunda stepped in and palmed the hinged door to the storage room, closing it. Irrwaer clutched her tally board, watching her yank a heavy box to block someone from coming in.

Oh, shit.

"So, I have a few questions for you, novice."

Of course, you do. The acolyte exhaled as strong bootsteps headed toward her and grappled with her courage. "And I have questions for you, Corpora."

"Oh? About what?"

Well, at least she wanted to play.

"Will you be allowed to return and communicate with your Lead while she is here?"

The warrior slowed her motions, perhaps in surprise, but now stood very close. Jaunda dropped her voice for privacy, leaning in to crowd her mark. "Not at will. If I'm summoned by a Priestess, maybe. Or sent by the Prime."

Irrwaer had gone beyond biting her lip to chewing it. Jaunda seemed amused by that but also mildly sobered by her own answer. She wasn't pleased with leaving D'Shea here for a turn or more to give birth.

"What if ..." Irrwaer began.

Jaunda leaned closer. "If?"

"What if Juliran authorized me to make a trade with you? An act for an act?"

The Corpora huffed through her nose, conveying all her skepticism for deals with the Sanctuary in one breath. Irrwaer was certain that sentiment should be returned in full, but she worked off what Juliran had taught her.

Prove useful to a Sister, and you will see her again.

That could be a warning or a promise.

She waited, tapping her tally board with her splinted charcoal. At first, Jaunda didn't reply.

Then, "Talk."

"Tarra," she began, "the Priestess you caught me with, forced me to show her where we'd be keeping D'Shea most of the time. She knows about an alternate approach, a way in without using the hall."

"Not surprised. Wonder why she's getting herself involved?"

"She's ambitious." Irrwaer shrugged. "An arcane sorceress first, like your D'Shea, then joined the Priesthood and became one of the youngest to bear a Sathoet."

"Ugh," Jaunda remarked.

Yeah, we're in agreement there. Except Irrwaer needed a son to rise above the status of a mere servant. *Focus.*

"If you'd like to know more about what she does, or which other Priestesses come sniffing around —"

The Red Sister grimaced. "That's not really my drive."

"But your elders might want to know, yes? You'll benefit from providing them with this intelligence, won't you?"

Jaunda looked at a random spot on the ground when she shrugged. Irrwaer almost couldn't believe it, but … *No. They don't care.*

Or, at least, it wasn't part of the Corpora's objectives.

Well, Tarra was an inconvenient obstacle anyway.

Irrwaer offered her original bait. "What about my bringing you to communicate with D'Shea when you need to? For any reason except escape, using the same secret passage?"

The Corpora considered it, for this was more to her liking. Before suggesting either way, however, she asked, "And what 'act' do you want in exchange?"

Oh, goddess …

Irrwaer turned her charcoal around in her sweating fingers. "Hm. I aim to become the Priestess-healer of this infirmary after Juliran. She is training me to take her place."

Jaunda looked confused. "Good for you?"

"But I must bear a Grandson of Braqth to become a Priestess."

She wrinkled her nose. "Yeah, I know."

Irrwaer exhaled more harshly than she meant, tamping down frustration and embarrassment. "And I have avoided *anyone's* bed. I have never …"

The Corpora stared at her.

"But that cannot last for me," she insisted, doggedly pursuing her logic. "I would rather my first rut *not* be on an altar facing down a demon summoned from the Abyss."

Jaunda was still staring.

Her armpits damp, Irrwaer growled, tapping her toe. Then the Red Sister took a step back, lifting her hands. The earlier sneer had become a warped grin.

"Wait. Are you … suggesting we trade a fuck for each time I see D'Shea?

You want me to fuck you. That's it?"

No!

"That's *not* it," she retorted hotly, pointing with her writing tool. "I need you to *train* my body. I've heard you have a false phallus you use from the 'top'? Not underneath, like a bua."

Jaunda's grin widened with an air of disbelief. "Yeah. I have one." She rubbed her jaw. "You … want me to train you. Train your slit."

No backing up now. Irrwaer swallowed. "I don't care about pleasure, but I need experience with male coupling, and I *need* endurance to live past my Priestess trial. I cannot wait too long."

"Aren't there plenty of swinging pricks in this place to practice with?"

"I don't want one from *here*. I want one that knows what she's doing and goes away afterward. One who *doesn't* belong to his mother. That's *you*, Corpora."

Jaunda guffawed then covered her mouth. Her eyes twinkled in the dark as she brought her hand down. "Can't say I don't grasp your reasoning, but I'm fucked if this is what I thought would be your deal."

Riddled with tension, Irrwaer waited again as the Red Sister took her time pondering.

Finally, she blurted, "Well?"

"Gonna need to think about it."

"What?!"

Jaunda grinned, lifting her gloved finger to place it on the acolyte's lips. "Shh. I mean, yeah, I'll trade this, but I need to think how to do it. To train a Sanctuary slit. I don't think you could handle the Cloister regime. I'm gonna have to bring it down a bit or, you know, you won't be able to sit next to your patients."

Irrwaer pursed her lips, quelling a rising tremor. "Very well."

That's a yes. Don't panic. She said yes.

"So," Jaunda continued, "how do I come by for 'training' without letting the whole Sanctuary know you're getting your fields plowed for later?"

Her face heated enough to light the darkness. The Corpora enjoyed this exchange far too much.

And we haven't even started!

"Good question," she admitted. "Juliran had a plan."

But as soon as she started to explain, the Corpora shook her head, rejecting it. "How about a message pellet? You use those?"

"No, I have an urgency ring, that's all."

"No worries, I get standard issue. Don't worry about getting me in. I'll get close enough, and you'll hear my voice in your ear. Then you choose the place to meet at the time. Deal?"

Irrwaer exhaled. "Deal."

"Good. Now just don't betray it, we'll be fine."

She frowned. "Why would I? I need this more than you do."

"Heh. Knew there was something off about you. I like it." Jaunda glanced over her shoulder. "Hm. We better get back so I can talk with the Lead before I go."

The tall Davrin moved the heavy box like it was nothing.

"Wait, didn't you have questions?" Irrwaer asked.

"Seems like I have more time to ask 'em." The Red Sister winked. "And that part about not caring about pleasure? We'll see about that."

Irrwaer's shoulders slumped as the enforcer stepped out. *You're wrong. It's not up to you.*

So confident, though. How would Jaunda react when she failed?

I don't care, as long as she teaches me what I need to endure conceiving my son.

With arms clutching herself, Irrwaer stared at the scrying panel in Juliran's personal quarters. She studied D'Shea as their new, long-term resident paced her small room, long, white shift rippling behind her.

"Do you have her uniform, Priestess?" she asked.

Juliran shook her head. "The High Priestess claimed it after we searched her. She will hold it until we have the baby, then both D'Shea and her uniform will be returned to the Red Sister Prime."

The acolyte frowned. "Did the Conceiver want to come instead? Is that why the High Priestess seemed irritable to be there?"

"Ah, very good. Yes, if Roshen didn't perform the task, Wilsira gladly would have. I am glad she did not." Juliran paused and looked up from fussing with her potions and balms. "Now we have time, what did Tarra tell you? And how long before did she arrive?"

Irrwaer recited the series of questions and her answers to the best of her memory. "She entered the infirmary just ahead of you. Not even half a mark. Her questions only seemed odd to me until then."

"Ah-ha, then Tarra caught the scent only when Lead D'Shea was brought in for questioning. Or, perhaps when I was summoned to perform the examination, as the sorceress has been hiding her condition for almost a turn."

Irrwaer cleared her throat. "I'm curious. Do you know whom she chose as sire?"

Juliran blinked at her with a widening smile. "Oh, you've already felt his aura, acolyte."

"The Headmaster? I thought so."

"It does seem obvious, although I don't know the last time he helped quicken a child." Juliran pondered. "It is interesting to see proof that he still *can*, even with a sorceress half his age."

"Huh? How old is he?"

Juliran smirked. "Didn't you notice he's a pure blond?"

"Well, Jaunda kept me from studying them."

"Right. We'll get to her. To answer your questions, he is older than me, than Wilsira, even older than Roshen."

Irrwaer shook out her ears. "Wait, alright ... Who is *older* than him?"

The Priestess had to think about that.

"The Valsharess?" the cait guessed.

"Oh, of *course*, Her. She's Eldest of us all. Hmm. Maybe the Prime Red Sister, as well."

Another pause. Irrwaer had to remember to blink. "Is that all? Two females in all of Sivaraus?"

"I believe so. If you aren't counting the Driders."

"Ugh," Irrwaer groaned to remember *them*.

Yet still, to think of one male being allowed to live so long. It wasn't chance. The Valsharess protected him, but only him, from the other arms of the city's power.

Juliran chuckled indulgently, reaching to caress Sil's silky head when the bua appeared from his room next to her workbench. "This seems like a good time to practice the calming technique, the three of us. You may need it if D'Shea gets her hands on you among your duties, the same as my child will need it when he's grown."

Irrwaer watched as Sil wrapped his arms around his Mother's hips, turning his face where the apprentice couldn't see. She looked back up. "Do you truly think she will try to escape?"

"No, I do not. But neither would I assume anything about what she knows or how she plans to use it. The sorceress and I were born less than a decade apart, and yet I do not truly know where she came from."

Irrwaer pursed her lips. "I was going to ask if there'd once been a House D'Shea?"

"Informally. Varessa D'Shea has always been at the Palace, never part of a separate House. No Matron claimed her, though some might have liked to. She was at Court long before I arrived at the Sanctuary, a born scholar with potent abilities, learning from any scroll, book, or codex she could seize."

Irrwaer frowned. "The Sisterhood chooses scholars?"

"Not usually, no. Something happened which got the Prime involved." Juliran paused then shrugged. "I only assume Varessa D'Shea survived whatever trial she was put under because she returned as a Red Sister and hasn't lived in the Palace since."

But she would live in the Sanctuary until she gave birth. *Hm.*

"How often do we see Red Sisters here?" Irrwaer asked.

"Oh … every two or three decades, perhaps." Juliran rubbed Sil's back, giving it a pat. He hadn't let go or made a peep. "None have been boarded here more than once, and thus far, all have been far younger than D'Shea."

Strange.

But only because she couldn't see all the threads which made the web, nor what had set the anchors and waited to rush in.

"So," Juliran said, "will we see the Corpora again as well?"

Irrwaer blinked, her face flushing warm. "Oh, um, yes. She agreed. She liked the simple trade."

"I thought that she would. Good."

"And I have a good hint from the Corpora that neither the Prime nor Elder Rausery are interested in using her to snoop much on us."

"I believe it. Among the Sisters, D'Shea herself is usually who you need to worry about gaining informants." The Priestess tapped her son's shoulder before pulling his reluctant arms free from her. "Come, then. Let us practice the calming aura together."

Irrwaer watched as Sil smiled and clasped his Mother's hand.

"Then we'll go over our new routines and contingencies for the infirmary," her Priestess said. "I'll teach you how to give Jaunda sight and sound access without passing weapons or tools to her superior."

CHAPTER 4

Psst. I'm here.

Irrwaer jumped and spun around, searching the stacks of bedding for the imposing figure.

She was alone.

Oh, yes. So that's what the pellet sounds like.

Only then did the acolyte realize she couldn't answer without a message spell of her own; she couldn't tell the Red Sister where to meet her.

Stupid oversight.

Or was it? Jaunda had said not to worry about getting her in; she'd be close.

Then I choose the place to meet. Hm.

Actions would speak as well as words, wouldn't they?

Irrwaer stepped out of the bedding closet, looking both ways down the drab-stone hall. There were small stacks of crates and baskets waiting to be sorted, some sweeping and cleaning supplies leaning against a door frame. There were feet walking about, work being done, but the fifth floor was peaceful at the moment.

That always changed, one way or another.

Irrwaer took a deep breath, opting out of silence, and strode confidently the full length of the hallway in both directions, glancing down each intersection as it curved or turned sharply. The Red Sister wasn't visible anywhere, but Irrwaer had that familiar sense of being watched.

Alright. Keep watching.

Irrwaer navigated the couple clusters of servants she encountered, providing them their next chores, then double-checked that her current patients were shut and locked in.

At last, she ambled down a lesser-used corridor with a recently cleaned closet she knew was large enough to contain a working table and chair. She stepped inside, closing but not locking the door, and sat in the fiberstalk chair to wait.

Jaunda did not waste time.

The tall Sister slipped in and reclosed the door, scanning the space, her hand signing, ★Good work.★

Irrwaer swallowed but dipped her chin. Jaunda secured the door to her liking, which included a sound ward created from an item she carried rather than a spell, and Irrwaer started to stand.

★No, wait as you are.★

Her rear end settled back into the chair, and Jaunda strode up to her, reaching for something on the back of her black belt which held a small armory and apothecary of items.

"Here, hold this," she whispered, dropping something long, cool, and floppy into Irrwaer's hands.

"What … ?"

She squeezed it, felt it give under the pressure but rebound an instant later. Her fingers recognized the false phallus before her eyes did.

Ugh.

Irrwaer grimaced, already knowing this would feel cold, blunt, and empty inside. The design was odd, though. Instead of a jutting cylinder with a thicker place to grab at the base, it curved like the bend of an arm before ending in a blunt bulb.

With hard leather shifting along with the *tink* of light metals, Jaunda had loosened her red leathers while the acolyte was distracted by the toy. When she pushed down her pants with one, eager shove, Irrwaer jerked her eyes back up only to stare at the white bush and pouting netherlips of a cait. The thick musk struck her nose a flick later.

She smells like an animal.

"Wanna kiss it?" Jaunda asked, reading her face with a soft chuckle. "No, huh? Heh. Maybe later, we have work to do. Gimme that."

The Red Sister took back her toy from Irrwaer's loose hands and spread her stance as far as her pants would allow. Her thick thigh flexed, and the acolyte accepted that she'd never outrun this Davrin or escape any hold involving those muscles clamping down on her.

Jaunda licked her fingertips and rubbed her slit enough to prove she was already wet from the anticipation, and Irrwaer watched as she pressed the base bulb of the phallus at the entrance of her body. She pushed it in with a grunt, lodging it in place and bringing her legs together. Now she looked like a cait with a cock, albeit obviously fake and wobbling.

The acolyte nodded, drying damp palms on her thighs. "Very clever."

"Not done yet, priestlet," she said tightly before speaking a magical command with a low, growling precision.

Irrwaer was unprepared and didn't catch the words. "What — ?"

Subtle illumination rushed from the Red Sister's core between her legs to the tip of her phallus. The acolyte stared with her mouth open as the obvious separation between the toy and Jaunda's body vanished. The toy stopped looking fake, softening to appear like flesh, and Jaunda shuddered and hunched over, the cords on her neck standing up as she grimaced.

Is this expected? Or painful?

Then Jaunda wrapped her right hand around her new appendage, stroking from base to tip to base again, and tilted her head back on an exhale. The grimace was gone, and the bliss on her face answered Irrwaer's worry.

*Expected. Decidedly **not** painful.*

"There," the Red Sister rasped, reaching with her left hand to snatch the loose bun at the back of Irrwaer's head.

"Hey, no, wait — !"

"Easy, sweetmeat. How's that?"

The acolyte had expected a rude and blunt phallus to be pushing at her lips, but she stilled again to feel incredible smoothness and … *heat*. The warmth of life caressed the side of her face, and the texture could convince her this phallus belonged to a born bua.

And the scent … *Impossible.*

In this short time, the toy had adopted a similar aroma to its wearer's slit.

Jaunda was grinning down at her. "Whatcha think? Good enough to stretch out your lurking cunt and get it prepped for the altar?"

Irrwaer shivered and nodded. *At least it won't be cold and dead.* She pointed to one side. "I can … bend over that table?"

"Not so fast."

The Red Sister reached for another item she'd kept at the small of her back. Irrwaer's eyes widened as she recognized a rough twine ball gag often used to quiet especially loud sacrifices so the room could hear the chants. She knew they were rough on the tongue and mouth so felt a very odd gratitude to witness Jaunda also tugged out a cloth to bind coarse fibers with something softer.

Wait.

"I don't need that," she said.

"You will." With a brief, idle stroke of her new cock, Jaunda shrugged. "Or if you wanna go bare-mouthed, fine. But you should know my sound dampening wards don't last forever and weaken as things get louder. The servants on this floor could hear your cries in a half-mark or could even lead that prying Lelinahdara where she'll see what I'm doing to you."

Panic burst through her middle. "So, the … quieter I am, the longer the ward lasts at full strength?"

The familiar grin returned. "You got it."

Irrwaer snatched the gag, latched her teeth onto the soft-wrapped ball, and brought it behind her head, fumbling with the simple rings and straps. Chuckling, Jaunda reached and took over to secure it for her.

"There. Nice and tight."

The acolyte breathed quickly through her nose. *Now what?*

The Red Sister decided for her, gripping her upper arms and pulling her out of her seat. Irrwaer expected to be pushed over to the table and shoved onto it; she did not expect Jaunda to trade places with her and take the seat herself.

"Down," Jaunda commanded, pulling one arm down and across her lap.

"Put your belly on my cock."

What?! Why?

So weird.

Irrwaer obeyed, settling onto her front across the Red Sister's lap, her toes touching the floor, her head hanging down, and her bottom pointed up. Jaunda arranged her a bit, shifting her weight so her abdomen and one muscular thigh mashed a hot erection between them.

"Mmm," she purred in her throat, caressing Irrwaer's buttocks.

She mumbled through her gag, trying to ask how Jaunda would enter her slit from this angle, when she remembered she could still hand sign.

"I'm not," the Sister answered aloud.

Helpful.

Then Jaunda lifted the acolyte's robes high, tucking them up under the sash at her waist to expose her legs and backside. Irrwaer seized hold of the chair's legs, her arms rigid as she looked over her shoulder. The Corpora smirked and winked.

"You wear small pants, huh?" she remarked, tugging curiously at the neutral, plain-woven briefs which kept her thighs from chafing. "Not flattering."

"*Mmbflb,*" Irrwaer responded, sucking air in through her nose when the warrior cait yanked them down over her ass. "*Waht —* !"

The Red Sister didn't wait but jerked them down, once on each side until her short pants dropped and settled at the crook of her knees.

"There we go. I knew it. You hide a pretty ass."

Irrwaer growled, signing, ★You won't arouse me prodding and poking with your fingers, Red Sister. I hate pawing like that!★

"Good to know."

Jaunda further explored Irrwaer's private cleft, caressing with her palms and spreading her open to look closer but did not use her fingers. For that reason alone, this didn't quite feel like the intrusive "health verification" she'd received upon moving to the Sanctuary.

But it's still wasting time.

Jaunda slapped one buttock, and Irrwaer yelped through her gag. The magical cock twitched under her weight as the sting spread across her skin.

"Oo, tender," the Red Sister cooed before repeating the slap with the same hand in the same spot.

Ow!

A third, identical slap, and Irrwaer squealed.

Fuck! What is she doing?

Slap!

What am I doing?!

Slap!

This was really starting to hurt!

She was somehow relieved when Jaunda switched her abuse to the other cheek, repeating the punishment, but that feeling faded as the Red Sister gradually heated that expanse of skin as well. The acolyte writhed in her lap. Once, she tried to evade that stinging palm before a strong arm wrapped securely around her waist.

"Good cait," the Red Sister huffed, "keep tight hold on that chair."

Irrwaer had the chair legs in a death grip. Although several of Jaunda's tools were within reach, it hadn't occurred to her to go for them.

That would only make this worse.

Slap!

"*Wrflm!*"

Finally, Jaunda leaned back, her breath shuddering oddly as she ground her toy up against the acolyte's sweaty abdomen. Irrwaer stared at nothing, both amazed and baffled how her buttocks felt seared, raw, and battered, yet … not injured enough to require her own skills.

Not nearly.

She heard Jaunda tug off her leather glove and jumped when she felt fingertips gently inspecting her netherlips. "*Mgm!*"

"Huh. A little sweaty. Alright, we can do better."

Better?

The enforcer reached over the acolyte's hips for something in a pouch on her sagging belt. "Hold on … there we go."

Uh-oh.

Jaunda caressed her smarting ass with her one gloved hand. "Still tingling? Or has it settled to a warm glow?"

Irrwaer made a face over her shoulder, signing, ★Hurts.★

"Good. It's supposed to."

Jaunda touched something oblong, white, and about the size of a beetle to the tip of her tongue, as if wetting it and tasting it at the same time. As she smacked her tongue against the roof of her mouth, the chuckle that followed was wicked.

"Oh, yeah. Good batch. This'll be fun."

Huh? What'll be 'fun'?!

That's when she felt Jaunda pry her cheeks open with the thumb and forefinger of her gloved hand then push whatever she'd just licked against her netherhole. Irrwaer's pucker clenched in surprise, but Jaunda was ready for that. She held the slippery thing in place until the shock had passed, inserting it just as the tight ring had finished flexing. Her bare finger followed the unknown object through the tight opening, nudging it deep into her rectum.

"*Mmgflptz!*"

Irrwaer clamped down on the invaders as Jaunda snickered and waited, holding her finger inside until the acolyte stilled.

What in the goddess damn did you — ?

She could feel the suppository dissolving, tingling, then beginning to warm. Like her sensitive ass cheeks, her asshole started to burn and throb. Her vision blurred a bit, a mist seeming to obscure her clearest thoughts, and her grip on the chair legs weakened.

Oh, no.

Either a sedative or an enhancer. What was it? Would she fall unconscious, or would everything feel too strong? Would she remain aware at all, or would she be a pile of rags unable to know she was bleeding?

The next sound in her throat sounded too much like an angry whine even to her own ears, and she struggled to roll off Jaunda's lap.

"Easy, cait, we've still got a deal."

The Red Sister caught her and broke the fall to the floor as she stood up, adjusting her hold on the smaller cait to haul her to her feet. Irrwaer blinked desperately to clear her sight as her head swam. Jaunda held her tight against her, pressing her durable erection against her, nudging her gut through her robe.

"Hey. Hey?" The Corpora took hold of her chin again to lift it. "Listen."

She smiled. "It's only gonna last a mark, at most. You'll be awake but nice and relaxed. Maybe it'll help your pleasure if you let it, or maybe it won't, but I only give this to those who *want* me to fuck 'em. Helps make sure I don't hurt 'em."

I ... I don't understand ...

Taking her by the shoulders, Jaunda steered her toward the table then caught her as she tripped over her small pants around her ankles.

"Heh. Whoops." The Red Sister leaned down, tugged those free and stuffed them down Irrwaer's robe at the neck. "So we don't forget them."

The promised relaxation encroached further, but Irrwaer was still able to walk with Jaunda's guidance. She held herself up with palms on the table as the Corpora moved some stacks to the floor to make a little more space, then put her hand between the acolyte's shoulder blades and pushed.

"Lie down. Get comfy."

The hem of her robes was still tucked in her waist sash, and with her underpants gone, she was fully exposed as she bent over and rested on the sturdy table. She sighed. The time had come to let someone use her sheath to bring their pleasure while she waited on their peak.

At least I won't become pregnant.

Jaunda kneeled behind her, using the thumbs of both hands to spread her ass, her skin by turns sizzling and rushing with heat. The Corpora's tongue glided a couple times along her netherlips, her throat making odd noises suggesting she enjoyed it. Irrwaer supposed she didn't mind too much.

It was a little unclean, though.

Then that tongue stroked all the way up to swirl around the crinkles of her keenly altered netherhole. Irrwaer shrieked at the intensity through her gag.

"Whoa." Jaunda rested a bare hand on her ass and leaned to one side. "Was that good or bad?"

Irrwaer was shivering, her thoughts bleary and fumbling for the ground. *I don't ... I don't know!* She signed off the side of the table. *Not ... pain?*

"Close enough."

Jaunda licked her again and went farther, using everything from the breadth of her tongue to paint swaths of saliva to its tip wriggling in as if searching for that white drug she'd pushed inside. She *really* seemed to enjoy it, even using her fingers to gently tug her sphincter wider and lick deeper!

Gross! Enough with my ass, we had a deal!

These words failed to reach her lips, however, as Irrwaer lay pliantly atop the platform and waited for the Red Sister to fuck her.

My first time. My choice ...

Sort of.

Maybe the best to be had in Sivaraus for someone like me.

When Jaunda finally stood up, purring as much as ever, Irrwaer felt hard thighs on the back of hers as she huddled close against her, running the ready cock lengthwise along her slit and in the cleft of her ass.

Finally!

But when did it get so slimy?

Jaunda reached to settle the blunt head into place. For an instant, Irrwaer thought her aim must be off, until her own thoroughly explored pucker yielded with disconcerting ease, engulfing the first finger-length before she grasped the situation.

"*Mgbmph!!*" she protested through her spit-soaked gag, jerking her hand around. ★Wrong hole!★

"No, it isn't, sweetmeat," Jaunda groaned, penetrating deeper. "Heh! Wow ... oh, yeah ..."

Irrwaer's eyes grew wider as her netherhole stretched around what must be a pole twice as wide as the one she'd held in her hands. *Did she change out her tool when I wasn't looking?!*

"Easy, breathe slower through your nose. You're doing fine."

She'd been spraying spit around her lips, trying to breathe through her mouth for some asinine reason. The acolyte had enough willpower left to take the advice and focus air through her flaring nostrils. Meanwhile, Jaunda eased the phallus deeper into her bowels, pausing whenever her netherhole spasmed, gradually increasing the strain on the overstretched pucker.

Eventually, Irrwaer felt Jaunda's thighs against the backs of hers.

Again.

There, the Corpora stopped, holding herself in place and expelling a deep, satisfied sigh.

Oh, Goddess … !

The Red Sister heard her whimper and leaned down to rest her chest on Irrwaer's back, keeping the magical tool fully embedded in the acolyte's waste hole. The enforcer reached to tuck a loosened lock of white hair behind her ear before speaking quietly into it.

"I'll get to your slit, priestlet. Next time or maybe some time after that. But right now, if I get to break someone in, I always take their ass first. You want to know why?"

Irrwaer blinked as the larger cait drew her phallus back only to the point where she had the urge to void herself then pushed it back in. Faster this time. It glided.

Still slimy.

"*Uhm*," she mumbled, lifting her fingers. ★Why?★

"Because if they don't feel pleasure, they always feel *this* in one way or another."

Jaunda gave her another partial draw-out then bucked back in before she spoke again. Irrwaer sucked in a breath.

"And if their heads hold together beneath me a couple of times, then the slit is an easy, easy ride. Nothing to fear, novice."

The Red Sister huffed a laugh before she groaned, cycling her rod in and out. A little faster, a little shallower. Irrwaer felt her open ring getting hot.

"Mmm. You never know. It might even feel better … than it would have, *ahhh* … if I'd *started* with that hole."

As Jaunda fucked her, Irrwaer continued to make noises aroused most from bursts of sensation and the sustained pressure of feeling so full, but she managed no other protest. Her body remained relaxed, her mind awake and aware of every stroke while the Red Sister rutted the tighter hole with contentment.

This act still trained her body to accept coupling with a male.

Just as I asked.

Her loosened pucker shifted from being warm and sensitive to overheated and numbed by the friction. Only as Jaunda's breathing changed, as the tempo of her thrust accelerated, did Irrwaer become aware for the first time of a point of no return. There was a moment when the phallus-bearer would grip her, cling to her, and keep humping until they reached that peak of ecstasy for which they had worked.

Jaunda had reached it.

"Aarrrrghh!" she groaned through her teeth, muffling herself by taking a bite on the lump of cloth stuffed down the back of Irrwaer's robe. "Yeah ... ! *Yeah ... ! Ohhh ... Rrrr ...*"

The warrior's heavy weight rested upon her, and a heart pounded powerfully against her back while labored breath rushed past her ear. Without releasing Irrwaer from her position, the Red Sister's hips shifted with her stance, and the acolyte felt the large phallus at last pulled from her body.

Suddenly, she was vacant.

I did it.

She'd coupled with another Davrin. Not what she'd *expected* this first time, but ... *This was fucking, nonetheless.*

"I'll get us some water," Jaunda whispered, nipping her earlobe on her way upright. "You should be alright by the time we get cleaned up, then you take me to D'Shea."

Irrwaer languidly flopped her hand. ★Yes.★

The Red Sister wouldn't be gone long, so she must have already known where to find the washing water. Undisturbed until then, Irrwaer would lie on her belly, floating in the aftermath as her gaping netherhole twitched, instinctively clenching itself shut. It took little effort for Irrwaer to recall the sensation of another being present inside her.

She wondered if it would last.

Curious and a little more alert, she reached down to touch the folds between her legs then rubbed her slippery fingers together.

Hm. Wet.

Was that residue from Jaunda's cock?

Or ... is it me?

"Irrwaer?" her Priestess whispered.

Juliran had caught her shoulder when she'd tipped a bit too far and prevented her from bouncing into the wall.

"I'm fine, Priestess."

Her elder glanced behind them at the patients, picked up a basket of her own and tossed her chin toward the door. They paused to secure the Davrin inside then moved to a small room Juliran used as an office. A few extra steps, and it could be as private and well-lit as her own quarters.

"I am sorry I missed the first exchange," she began without preamble. "You seem to have taken something. Tell me what happened."

Ughhh ...

"First, we both got what we wanted, my Priestess. And your method to let Jaunda speak with D'Shea without touching her worked just fine."

"Excellent on both counts. Am I wrong, though? Are you just tired?"

Irrwaer swallowed. "The Red Sister did give me something to help me relax."

"Can you describe it? What did it taste like?"

The acolyte snorted unexpectedly and covered her mouth. Her face was hot as her Priestess frowned with disapproval. "Apologies, Priestess. Um. A white pellet shaped like a grub. I didn't swallow it, I don't know what it tastes like. But it dissolves with body heat and encourages blood flow on contact."

Irrwaer thanked Braqth that Juliran put it together herself. "Ah. Which orifice?"

Sigh.

"My netherhole. Which is where she wanted to start."

Juliran bit her lower lip as if to hold back a grin; she nodded. "I have heard that is more common in the Sisterhood."

"What? Why?"

"Probably because every Davrin has one. I assume you're not terribly damaged?"

She shook her head and looked down. "No."

"Generous of her. Do you want me to look?"

Irrwaer covered her rear with her hands. "No!"

"Very well." Juliran considered further. "The training is useful, Irrwaer. Sometimes the demons try for the netherhole."

"They do?"

"Yes. If they succeed and spurt there, they must stay longer as the acolyte tries again." The corners of Juliran's mouth tightened. "It's a constant battle of wills. Some hopefuls have been on the altar for several marks, through multiple ruts, trying to control their summoned sire. In my view, all the better if you're prepared for the possibility. He's less likely to wrest control from you."

"Excellent," Irrwaer grumbled in irony, glaring at the corner of the desk. "But moving on, how was the visit with D'Shea afterward?"

The acolyte shrugged. "As I said, it worked. Jaunda placed her bare hands on the runes like I showed her, and she was able to see and hear her Lead on the other side of the wall without stepping through."

"Hm. Did she try to convince you to open the door?"

"Yes. She failed."

"Very good. And what did they talk about?"

Here, Irrwaer grimaced but met her superior's calm gaze. "They spoke in a cant. I understood the words, but they lacked context."

"Unsurprising. I suppose I'd have been disappointed if they spoke plainly. Did you take any notes?"

Irrwaer nodded, reminded only then to pull the scrap of parchment from her pocket and hand it over. "I had to rewrite from memory after Jaunda left. She searched me and took the notes I made at the time."

Chuckling, Juliran accepted the note, opening it to read by heatless candlelight. "Hm. Be mindful of any sense of urgency as they speak. Let us see how often the Corpora arrives, and what she does to pass contraband or convince you to give her physical access. Call me at the slightest concern."

"Yes, Priestess."

Irrwaer stood awkwardly, trying to decide if there was anything else she should share about Jaunda. Juliran noticed and shrugged.

"Did you enjoy it?" she asked and watched her apprentice purse her lips.

"I don't know," Irrwaer admitted. "Could have been worse?"

"A good sign, then." Juliran smiled wider. "I'm almost certain the Corpora sees you as a challenge. I've heard she can be brutal with that phallus, but you are apart from her standing orders with her elders, so you may be seeing her as few other 'receivers' do. Appreciate your luck, child, don't dismiss it."

Irrwaer took a deeper breath, her middle quivering at how easily she still recalled the Red Sister rutting her for pleasure.

Only for pleasure, it seemed. Nothing else.

"Yes, Priestess. I shan't."

CHAPTER 5

IT SEEMED EVERY PRIESTESS IN THE SANCTUARY WOULD COME TO VISIT THEIR FLOOR over the next quarter turn. Most only wanted to confirm the rumors or gawk at the Red Sister's swelling belly; some tried to stab deep with taunts and contempt while they were there. All of them arrived, conveniently, when their resident needed her exercise outside the small room which kept her hidden and protected from prying eyes and fingers.

Irrwaer had always used her panic ring more often to alert about the other Priestesses than she had for help with unruly patients. This didn't change even with Jaunda added to the mix, but the frequency grew tenfold.

"Ahh, Irrwaer. Long-time, no-see?"

"Acolyte. I require your assistance."

"Acolyte Irrwaer. My Priestess sent me on her behalf ..."

"I've heard you already know she'll squirt a cait! Is that true?"

Ugh ...

Her rounds became longer and longer as she had to check and set twice as many wards farther out to give her and Juliran more warning when someone arrived on the floor.

Conniving cunts.

Thankfully, Irrwaer's Priestess had received exemption approval from High Priestess Roshen from all ritual obligations during the time D'Shea was here. Juliran was nearly always present to assist with infiltrator control or when voices or bodies in the hallways grew lively.

The Priestess-healer had also obtained more Palace guards assigned to the infirmary floor by petitioning the Valsharess, and she'd taken to locking Sil in her private quarters so Irrwaer wasn't responsible for him as well. They had even made sure their Reveries were staggered so one of them was always awake on the fifth level of the Sanctuary.

Maddening.

Half our cycles are spent managing the presence of guards and dissuading intrusive loiterers! Why are they even interested? Who is this scholar-turned-Red-Sister?

The two Priestesses who *hadn't* shown up yet were Lelinahdara and Wilsira the Conceiver, but that was only a matter of time. That Tarra was staying away was no doubt a sign of biding her time.

Perhaps she's waiting on Wilsira to act.

Meanwhile, Jaunda had arrived about every other span to pull Irrwaer into a storage closet and gag her, though she seemed to know she couldn't keep the acolyte to herself as long as she'd like.

Nonetheless, the Sanctuary cait cooperated as the Red Sister donned her phallus and inevitably fondled the other cait's netherhole, preparing it with that oily, warming anal pellet. Sometimes the stinging spanks accompanied the preparation, sometimes it was only during the rut itself, like an afterthought.

There were new touches to her body, however, either before or during the rut. Jaunda's bold, inquisitive hands focused on tender folds and sensitive bumps hidden beneath the healer's furry muff; on her easily palmed breasts and long, tweakable nipples; and further exploring responses in her back, belly, and ears. Pain was often involved but not always.

Whichever way their tryst went, Jaunda seemed so intrigued by various bits and colors and scents of her skin. She drank in the sounds and squeaks Irrwaer made from pure reaction to how her body was used. For ending their engagement with her pleasure peak, however, the Red Sister chose only the acolyte's asshole.

Through her first four couplings, Irrwaer still didn't know what a prick in her slit felt like. She was starting to care less about that, however, as the young healer remained alert through all of it: aware how much she relaxed, and how readily her body yielded to direct penetration. She grew familiar with the sense of fullness, with Jaunda's grunts and breathing, and gained insights on her preferences and paces.

In the end, Irrwaer was oddly content when the Red Sister found those couple of moments of ecstasy in humping her backside. With Jaunda in her throes unaware of her surroundings at all, each of them could focus on the tight grip of flesh around her slick member.

Almost like a small altar ritual ...

At the end of each encounter, Irrwaer confirmed her slit had generated its own lubricant, as if anticipating another phallus to follow the Sister's. The source was separate from that slickness which seemed to transfer from Jaunda's core arousal through the tip of her toy. Irrwaer never quite knew what to do with any of it except clean it off.

At least it was proof of her concept: that her body could be trained to become wet and pliant even if her mind was disengaged.

This will help me on the altar. I know it.

D'SHEA WAS OFTEN EATING WHILE SHE SPOKE WITH HER CORPORA THROUGH THE wall. By now, Irrwaer was certain much of their cant were updates of what was going on outside the Sanctuary, probably including a few simple instructions to assist the sorceress's influence outside her small room.

Some of it may be simple conversation.

To help keep the elder sane.

Who is she? Or was?

If there was no House D'Shea, no Matron D'Shea, why did so many females in the Sanctuary seem to take glee with her temporary imprisonment? How many enemies had she made?

At least Jaunda is loyal.

One eve, as Irrwaer and D'Shea were locked inside together while the former changed the bedding and bathing supplies, the Lead Sister caught the acolyte staring thoughtfully at her one too many times.

"Always a busy head for one so quiet," the sorceress remarked. "What's on your mind, Irrwaer?"

Only Juliran had ever asked before.

Irrwaer's back stiffened with wary concern, but then she shrugged, shaking out the new bedding before tucking it over the stuffed mattress placed atop the cot. As always, she took the opportunity to search it for hidden items. She heard the sorceress scoff.

"If I was going to hide a poison needle, it wouldn't be in a fiber stack where I might stick myself."

True. It would probably be in her hair, which was now loose and reached her mid-back. The pregnant mata had been allowed nothing but a simple shift, more for warmth than modesty; she was even barefoot. Irrwaer already knew how thorough the initial strip-and-search of patients was.

Because it must be.

D'Shea had been largely silent herself for spans now but perhaps this solitude was finally getting to her. Irrwaer wasn't sure if the Red Sister either knew or suspected the bloodstone inlays on the ceiling could absorb any words exchanged in this room and hold them for a time, long enough for Juliran to scry them when she woke. The apprentice wasn't going to tell the sorceress if she wasn't aware, but she would be surprised if D'Shea didn't at least suspect.

Take advantage. Tell her something.

"I was thinking that you seem to have no bloodline," Irrwaer said bluntly. "I'm wondering why you're so much work to keep safe."

D'Shea's jaw hardened, the insult clear. "Every mage has a bloodline, House or not. Mine is one of the strongest."

"I've heard, Lead. If your House is extinct, where did it reside? Which House pulled it down and assimilated it?"

The Red Sister's eyes narrowed, joined by a creeping smile that did nothing to ease Irrwaer's nerves. "It was never pulled down. The house still stands."

The acolyte frowned to show her confusion but said nothing, waiting for the sorceress to continue.

"No guesses?" D'Shea challenged her. "Or does a little 'priestlet' not listen to the whispers despite keeping so quiet?"

Priestlet. She must have heard that from Jaunda.

Irrwaer reflected mostly on Juliran's story as she knew it. "The Palace?"

D'Shea arched one brow, her strained features easing like web strands released from a spider's weight. "How's that your guess?"

The youth shrugged. "They say that was your last residence before joining the Sisterhood. That you were never seen anywhere else, and no Matron claimed you."

"Hm." The pregnant Davrin shifted her weight, cupping her rounded belly. "So, Juliran is doing her due diligence *and* sharing with you. That's interesting."

Irrwaer's mouth twitched with chagrin. "It suggested to me House D'Shea was kept close to the Queen."

Somewhat mollified, Varessa D'Shea nodded once.

"Why? Was it another scholar group, but for caits rather than the wizards in the Tower?"

Irrwaer received an acerbic glance as the sorceress arched her lower back, making her belly protrude ever farther.

"That answer actually makes sense," D'Shea remarked. "I might have preferred that being the reasoning."

The acolyte shifted uncomfortably when it became clear the sorceress wouldn't answer the question. Perhaps *because* it didn't make sense.

If the Valsharess wanted a bloodline of strong mages and scholars in Her Palace, why did She let House D'Shea die out?

As if the sorceress might have heard this thought, an invisible weight returned to the room as D'Shea took to her clean mattress. Her arms wrapped around her middle as if to hide what she'd shown blatantly a moment ago. She stared at the floor, or at a memory, before looking up.

"Sixth House, aren't you?" she asked. "Peniel. Known more for healers budding up among their mages."

Irrwaer bowed her head. "Yes, Lead Sister. The Matron is my aunt."

D'Shea nodded, her thoughts working hard behind dark, crimson eyes. "Have you felt your healer's aura open for Jaunda?"

Irrwaer blinked hard. "Huh?"

The sorceress smiled. "You could practice your focus with her, you realize. Instead of *lying* there, passive and mewling. She's mentally resilient and quite strong-willed. One of our best. She'd respond, and you wouldn't hurt her even if you give yourself a headache."

"Uhh ..." Irrwaer glanced at the door.

"Oh, does that make you uncomfortable? Odd. I know you've practiced with two others. Juliran and another one. Someone I haven't seen yet."

Sil.

"Excuse me, Lead, I have rounds to finish," she said, committing to the urge to leave immediately. "I'll bring your next meal at the usual time."

"Add a bit more, would you? I woke up hungry the last time."

"Yes, Lead."

The sorceress remained on her cot as Irrwaer went through the laborious steps to open the door the smallest bit, slip out, and secure it behind her in the hallway. She glanced at the two guards who flanked either side three paces away, both of whom saluted her. Shaking the subtle, creeping doubt out of her thoughts, the acolyte returned to her endlessly busy tasks, wondering if Juliran had woken up by now.

If she has, did she just watch me talk with the Sister? Will she listen in with the bloodstone?

Even if she did, the Priestess wasn't sure to enlighten her at once.

Chapter 6

Irrwaer awoke from Reverie with a start, instants before she heard the voice in her ear.

I'm here again, sweetmeat. Just outside.

Shit!

Her heartbeat kicked up strong as she bolted up and swung her legs over the side to stand. She only realized she hadn't checked her slippers for spiders as she dispelled her own ward and had her hand on the handle.

Fuck! Stupid!

She nudged the door open and signed, *Get in, get in quick!*

Jaunda's grin fixed in place as she signed, *Gladly.*

Irrwaer glimpsed out to check for clusters of servants as the Red Sister stepped past her, fortunately seeing none as she closed and secured the door. Jaunda took the liberty to set the sound-absorbing ward.

Then heavy, gloved hands fell onto her shoulders, and she hunched up as the enforcer leaned down to breathe in her ear.

"I have an appetite for fresh slit this eve."

Strong fingers slipped along her skin and hooked her sleep gown, stripping it off her shoulders.

Oh, Goddess, now?!

She wasn't ready!

Yet her arms stayed down, easing Jaunda's slow, steady drag of fabric down the lines of her body; the warrior indulged herself, massaging and squeezing soft flesh along the way.

"Step out," Jaunda commanded.

She did, watching her guest toss the gown aside. Irrwaer stood only in her slippers while the Red Sister ogled her.

"I really like that you don't wear the small pants anymore," she said, stroking her erection through her leather pants.

Irrwaer crossed her arms beneath her breasts. "Less benefit now, more risk to lose them as they're taken off all over the fifth floor."

Jaunda chuckled with immense satisfaction. "Except you aren't even wearing 'em here. I like it. Get on the bed. All fours, facing the wall."

Shit, shit.

Irrwaer obeyed, climbing with care onto the most comfortable place she'd be fucked yet. *In my slit, supposedly.*

But not before Jaunda fixed her ball gag on the acolyte and enjoyed an energetic round of slapping her ass to a heated glow. Irrwaer gripped her sheets and groaned as the blows came harder and faster than before, the sounds and pain interspersed with thumbs spreading her cheeks and a tongue on her netherhole.

Once her buttocks were hot and throbbing, the wet crinkle in between them had relaxed, fully expecting a larger prodding very soon. But then she felt a bare finger glide easily between her netherlips, smearing abundant lubricant over the folds before dipping into a *different* hole.

My cunt …

"Nice," Jaunda murmured. "Roll over."

"*M-mmgh?*"

"You heard me. Roll over. Onto your back. Spread your legs."

Irrwaer almost couldn't let go of the sheets, and a peep slipped out when her sensitive ass scraped against the bed, but she got into position. The Corpora eagerly hooked her hands behind her knees and tugged Irrwaer so that her ass rested on the very edge of her bed.

"*Yrghp!*"

"Oh, yeah."

Jaunda pushed her legs as wide as they would go, and Irrwaer bit down on her gag with a grimace. Before her vision cleared, the Red Sister had dropped to a knee; she ducked down, planting her mouth full on the wet sex.

"*Yii!*"

"Shh! Mm, yum."

Jaunda returned to sucking and nibbling on her with zeal while loosening her red leathers to release the erection already in place. Irrwaer could only stare down her naked belly, able to watch the warrior use her mouth like this for the first time. As with the initial coupling, she wasn't sure what she felt.

It still seemed a little unclean.

"Want the tranquil pellet up your ass again?"

The acolyte blinked, gradually absorbing the question. *She's ... ?*

She'd never given her the choice before.

Jaunda looked up to read her hand, obviously waiting for an answer.

Are you fucking it?

The Corpora grinned, tickling her pucker with a finger. "Maybe after."

The acolyte thought it over. *No. I will pass.*

She would try her first time without it.

"Right."

The strong cait returned to feasting with her nose pressed to her fur, teasing her netherhole to encourage more moisture. Irrwaer contemplated the quick flicks and gliding swirls of an unwary warrior who enjoyed this act whether the apprentice was squirming or not.

Does she truly like the taste?

With an excited growl, Jaunda planted both hands outside her hips and pushed herself up to standing, her leathers already pushed down to her thighs. Her umber-red eyes smoldered as her hands ran up Irrwaer's legs, positioning her calves to rest on her armored shoulders. The acolyte's mouth sagged around its gag to witness such exposed desire she'd only sensed and heard behind her before. In some ways, it was more intense than the first cock in her ass.

"*Mykf!*" she whimpered as Jaunda positioned the tip of her phallus in a softer, even more yielding place than her ass. She could squeeze down and tilt her hips to make entry much more difficult at the rear hole, she knew that now.

*But I can't ... **stop** ... this!*

With or without the drug, she was slick and open. Her pelvis could clench a little but not nearly enough to slow her trainer's progress as the magical cock stretched her new opening with embarrassing ease; it was being *swallowed* by it!

Jaunda groaned, long and low, as she leaned forward, bending Irrwaer's body up and bracing herself on her knuckles. "Shit, yeah, that's the stuff ..."

All the way in.

So easily ...

Then Jaunda withdrew her cock.

And leaned in again.

"Ah ... like silk, Irrwaer ..."

Silk?

And she used her name?

The Red Sister opened her eyes, caught her in a stare, and grinned as she pumped her hips faster, using the full length of her rod. Irrwaer stared back, her position even more helpless than bending over a table.

I can't look away while she does this. I see every tic, every grimace ... plain to see.

This was what it would be upon the altar.

Her cunt made a wet, squishing sound, and Jaunda answered with a grunt and harder pounding against her, against the mattress. Irrwaer just studied her face.

Oh, Goddess.

The Red Sister had been right. After expecting every visit to feel her pucker stretched out and rubbed raw, this *was* an "easy ride."

It feels different.

Not bad, but less intense. More relaxing.

You could practice your focus with her, you realize, D'Shea had said. *Instead of lying there.*

Passive and mewling.

Oh ... Goddess ...

The Corpora was huffing, working her slit hard and with greater abandon than she did her ass. Irrwaer fell into the rhythm, allowing her eyes to drift, to droop.

Focus.

Jaunda sucked air in through her teeth. "*Shhfff* ... ! Whoa."

The Red Sister's rhythm faltered. Then picked up again, and Irrwaer just barely felt it: a light mingling of their auras the more she relaxed. The more she became aware of her magic. Opening up.

Like when I practice with ... oh ...

She still felt no overt pleasures between her legs, but that didn't mean there wasn't pleasure within her. Elsewhere.

Everywhere.

All over.

"Mm ... mmhm!" Irrwaer groaned, her first sound of encouragement.

"Shhhit, yeah," Jaunda answered, her eyes wide and staring at her face like there was something new to see. "Do that ... s'more, healer ..."

Very well. Just don't stop if I do.

"Fffuck!" the Sister growled as sensation seemed to surge, nudging her hands against Irrwaer's waist, bracing herself again.

The acolyte watched her slippers bounce atop Jaunda's shoulders as the warrior wallowed with renewed fervor within the slit between tightly squeezed thighs.

*Between **my** thighs.*

A new, fresh, wet slit. A delightful challenge for the right Red Sister.

Where we are both rewarded.

Pleasure and magic hummed together. Jaunda's eyes grew unfocused yet her strength continued, unflagging. Irrwaer wasn't sure what was happening, as she wasn't quite *healing* the rutting fighter atop her.

But she was granting strength.

And *something* was rising.

Quickly!

"Oh! Yeahhh!"

Irrwaer's vision blurred as the crash of another's aura swept over her in their climax; she cried out through her gag. She was taken, held, and thrashed by the explosion of pleasure coursing through her guts, rushing through her limbs.

She wasn't aware of anything ...

Until Jaunda collapsed on top of her, shutting down her air.

"Mmfglfgg!" she complained, pushing at her, slapping the hard shoulder with an open hand.

"Sorry," the Corpora groaned, withdrawing her cock and falling backward onto the floor. "Whew! ... wow."

No sounds but the two of them catching their breath.

"Whatever you did just now, priestlet," Jaunda muttered, sounding on the verge of sleep. "I think that's how yer gonna make it ..."

Irrwaer let that sink into her muzzy thoughts.

Could she be right?

As Jaunda dropped into a doze, the acolyte removed her gag and sat up. She dared to imagine commanding the climax of a chained demon on the altar the way she'd just commanded a Red Sister to peak while fucking her on her bed.

To reach their ecstasy and share it with me, even if I cannot reach my own.

After exchanging such a gift, did the phallic one have no strength or desire left to harm her afterward? Was that how Juliran survived her trials?

Probably.

Which means I can, too.

Chapter 7

2890 S.E. – The Sanctuary of Sivaraus

"She's close," said her Priestess through a yawn after a long cycle of keeping order in the third-floor nursery while Irrwaer handled the fifth by herself. "Hm. The child is full size. The contractions can begin at any time."

Irrwaer nodded through her persistent headache, trying to sort through sensations of concern which had been building so gradually that she struggled for words to describe them.

"The Lead has not been resting well," she began.

"Of course. Common this close to birth."

The acolyte frowned. "Her Reverie seems plagued with dreams. She sometimes talks."

"Oh? What does she say?"

Irrwaer looked away. "Just ... protests. Babble."

Juliran hummed. "Many matas fear giving birth, Irrwaer. It is our pinnacle moment of vulnerability, the closest to death we are while young and strong. Always has been. Hide it as we might, this becomes obvious when the moment becomes real enough."

The apprentice sighed, trying to formulate what else was bothering her, what agitating vibrations in the web might be closely linked.

The Conceiver was a worrisome concern due to her absence as D'Shea's time in their custody approached its eventful closure. Wilsira had never arrived to observe or taunt D'Shea as they had expected, nor had Kerse set foot on this floor that Juliran could detect.

There had also been a brief visit from the Headmaster two spans ago. D'Shea did not tolerate his presence long before she demanded Irrwaer lead him away. Unlike when the mages had compelled the Driders away from the bodies on the dock, the sorceress's aura had been closed tightly against him.

That didn't go well.

Finally, there was Lelinahdara, who had convinced Juliran to accept re-payment for covering her son-less presence upon D'Shea's arrival. Tarra had granted assistance on the nursery, giving them both a break from the children when needed, as some of the future-consorts there grew larger and restless.

"They will be moved to the fourth floor soon enough," said the new Priestess. "I shall be governing there more in the future. It's just as well I get acquainted with them now."

"Reasonable," Juliran agreed, having already confirmed this. "I accept."

Tarra had stepped in as the youths' tutor thrice so far; two times before the Headmaster and one time after. Each time, she'd managed to catch Irrwaer's elbow before heading back to her quarters on the sixth floor.

"Isn't Sil supposed to be among his age-mates?" she'd asked the last time. "He's been absent each time I've come."

No doubt deliberate on Juliran's part.

Irrwaer had shrugged. "I forget to look for him when I do the head count. It is the privilege of his mother to place him where she will."

"Hm. So, it is. Does she always keep him with her? You know, like the Conceiver does Kerse?"

And completely unlike you. Where is your bua, anyway?

Irrwaer wrinkled her nose. "I don't know."

Tarra was incredulous. "How can you not? You're *always* here."

"Because I don't have access to *all* spaces here, and I have neither the time nor the care to spy on my Priestess spending time with her son."

"Hmph." The Priestess's smile was oddly sweet. "You are and have always been a most loyal and *desirable* servant for any Daughter of Braqth, Irrwaer. I'm certain this attitude will secure your future."

Irrwaer bared her teeth in a lackluster smile. "Thank you, Priestess. Please excuse me."

Now, between the Red Sister's restless dreams, her rejection of the chosen sire, the encroaching change of responsibility and routine with Tarra, the lack of the Conceiver providing so much as a blessing on the pregnant mata, Jaunda having not visited D'Shea in a while, and now Juliran seeming to change her mind about listening when Irrwaer sensed something was off, instead dismissing her and blaming it all on an agitated mother soon to give birth ...

"I have greater concern we are missing an imminent warning, Priestess," she finally said. "Should we not go over plans for when the birthing begins?"

Juliran frowned. "They're nothing unusual, Irrwaer. D'Shea will give birth in that room. We have access to everything we need on this floor. We have direct access through a private passage. We are prepared."

"I beg pardon, Priestess, but we are not prepared," the acolyte replied. "We skipped her last two examinations because of the rush of new poisonings. You haven't checked the bloodstone in the last three cycles, either. Anything that's been spoken there is already gone."

Juliran rubbed her brow, looking annoyed. "She's just waiting and eating, apprentice. As she has been for an entire turn."

You are not this stupid, Priestess!

Irrwaer bit her tongue and rubbed her brow as well. Her head ached and was making her irritable. She sensed movement in her periphery and glanced over to see Sil peeking out through a crack in his door.

Bad habit, bua, spying on your elders.

He met her gaze and stuck out his hand, signing that he needed to bring his chamber pot to the disposal.

Irrwaer backed up in her thoughts. Truly, how would he *avoid* witnessing things he shouldn't when the Priestess kept him so close? For that matter, how much did all the servants and demure sires overhear as their Matrons and mother and aunts discussed all the ways of running Sivaraus?

Few risk the punishment after watching what happens to those who expose their matrons' business.

"A moment, my Priestess," she said, "Sil needs cleaning."

Juliran stared at her workbench and didn't respond.

"Acolyte? Acolyte Irrwaer ..."

She hissed. "Sil. What are you d — ?"

When Irrwaer turned around, she nearly lost hold of her basket as a cold rush swept through her to see the look on his face.

"Something's wrong with Mother." The bua swallowed. "She can't hear me."

Shit.

Irrwaer shoved her mundane tasks into a closet and locked multiple doors before seizing the bua's arm and dragging him back to where he must have left another door open.

I hope he did ... I'm not sure I can get in!

Her relief felt tepid to confirm the door was cracked just wide enough for the child to slip through. At first, she was impressed he'd been able to use the runes and move it on his own.

But then, he just turned forty.

Irrwaer pushed it a little more to pull them both through, scanned the front room for disturbance, and secured the door behind them when it seemed clear. She smelled a vague, sickly scent in the air, and her chill coalesced into a rock in her stomach as she darted to the healer's bench to gather a few bottles and boxes.

Drugged or poisoned, no doubt.

Likely to distract from the imminent birth on their floor. She had a guess who but could easily be wrong. A Davrin of her station could make no accusations, could act on no suspicions.

What will become of me if Juliran dies now?

Sil followed on her heels as Irrwaer burst into her Priestess's bedchamber for the first time. The comforts expected for any Priestess were all present, most of it seemed decades old though still in good condition. The acolyte lit multiple candles, clearing all the shadows from the room, and checking the corners, closets, or any place a Sathoet could hide. She kept sniffing the air.

Just Juliran. Albeit not at her cleanest.

"Sil. Get a bucket of water from her bath."

"Yes, Acolyte."

The bua hurried away, and Irrwaer leaned over her mentor to take her vitals before pulling open the sweaty robes for a more thorough examination.

I need to check on D'Shea ...

But she couldn't be in two places at once, and the symptoms were just worrisome enough that she had work to do to stabilize Juliran before leaving anywhere.

Then what? Leave her alone with Sil? Drag the bua with me everywhere?

Irrwaer glanced at the scrying panel. She'd been the conduit a few times to help sustain it as Juliran listened to the echo of words contained by the bloodstone, but she only had a basic idea how to initiate it. And if something went wrong, she might be unconscious on the floor with Sil standing between her and his mother on the bed ...

No. I'll have to use the passage as soon as I can.

"Here, dunk this cloth," Irrwaer instructed Sil as he returned with fresh water from the spout. "Squeeze it like this and wipe her down to cool her skin. Repeat until you've covered the skin twice. Alright?"

He looked back and forth between them, uncertain.

"Sil!" she hissed. "You're a healer! Do you want her to die?"

He gulped, shook his head, and climbed onto the bed, careful to balance the water as he began dunking, squeezing, and wiping while the acolyte worked. As he drew the old scents away, the new ones in the sweat gave Irrwaer a few hints about what to try for a counter to the drug, something to neutralize it faster.

She mixed a fresh tonic after inspecting the components herself, trusting none of those prepared previously and sitting on the workbench. Juliran was unresponsive enough to risk choking if required to drink, so Irrwaer took inspiration from the Corpora.

Turning her Priestess on her side, Irrwaer inserted a squeeze vial into her netherhole. After several gushes, she had to plug her elder's body with a finger until the moisture passed into her blood. While waiting, she also noticed two odd puncture wounds in her left buttock like a giant spider bite.

"What are you doing?" Sil asked.

"Keep her cool, bua."

Once they had done all they could do, Irrwaer busied herself preparing a second dose if needed and scratching down her observations for later. Juliran's son settled down next to her with his chin on her shoulder and closed his eyes. Irrwaer was glad he could be still and quiet like that, though she looked up once or twice as she felt subtle hints of magic answering itself.

Hm. His aura seems to be helping.

She let him be, and within a fifth mark, the fever had broken. Juliran's pupils responded normally as the sweats stopped and her heart slowed down to normal.

Good.

"I need to check on a patient," Irrwaer said. "Do you want to come or stay here?"

The pretty bua blinked at the choices, frozen between them for a flick. "I-I'll stay with her."

"I won't be long. Don't touch anything, and do *not* answer anyone's voice, knock, or entrance. Stay silent. Hide if they try to come in."

"Yes, Acolyte."

Irrwaer hurried from the bedchamber to sitting area and on to the wardrobe, ducking behind numerous gowns and robes to find the latch that brought her to the passage where she'd often led Jaunda, though with her, they'd started closer to that first storage room where Irrwaer had bent over.

It was a longer, darker leg to reach the same place, but the acolyte held her breath and rushed on silent feet to the panel with the runes which allowed her to check in on their resident. She spotted scuffs and scrapes where they shouldn't be two strides before she reached the spot. Placing her bare hands against the wall, covering the runes and drawing her focus, Irrwaer saw one of the three images she had anticipated.

The waiting room was empty, though orderly and without destruction. Nothing inanimate was missing; Varessa D'Shea had simply been removed.

Taken.

IRRWAER WAS OVERWHELMED THROUGH THE NEXT CYCLE AS JULIRAN RECOVERED, attempting to do the minimum to keep order and convince the patients and guards that nothing was amiss. They noticed the pretty bua who came to get her twice, however, and the sense of concern which leaked from him started to spread.

"S-stay silent for now," the Priestess whispered, struggling with her own weakness and the horrifying news of the vanished Red Sister. "I will make a potion that will give me the appearance to reassure them."

With a swallow, Irrwaer nodded. "What do you remember, Priestess?"

A shake of her head. "Nothing after I meant to return to my quarters."

"I found a wound here." Irrwaer rubbed a spot on her own backside. "Could have been a glass fork made to look like a bite."

"Hm. Why?"

"Because there was a shard of glass left behind."

"Ah." Juliran blinked. "Then I don't know how I made it to my bed."

Sil spoke up then. "I heard someone outside my door, Mother. I thought it was Irrwaer. When she left, I noticed the smell, and you couldn't hear me."

The females stared at him, each needing several moments to decide whether they wished to believe him. Could he be mistaken? If not, someone had just walked in?

She must have.

One Priestess to take *her* Priestess out of the game when their most important patient and link to their current status was most vulnerable.

Quite the moment to reveal someone could have entered this private space at any time.

Irrwaer considered the scrape and scuffs revealing the presence of someone before her in the passage. *Claws, perhaps?* That another Priestess was involved was a given, but the one most likely to bring him on an abduction was the one Priestess they had yet to see.

We still haven't.

By the passing moods on Juliran's face, she'd probably come to similar conclusions, holding all the same worries in both hands.

"Come here, Sil," she said, opening her arms.

He responded at once, falling into her embrace.

"We'll get everything in order," the lead healer said, her lips touching silky white hair. "Keep our ears alert. If nothing is discovered or revealed in one more cycle, I will report to the High Priestess."

Irrwaer watched them hold each other. Although Juliran had another son somewhere in the Sanctuary, a half-blood Davrin kept in a chamber designed to hold his kind, Juliran seemed to cling to her second son as if he was all she had left in Sivaraus.

"Yes, my Priestess," she said.

"Here, let me teach you how to check the bloodstone," Juliran said. "It's not difficult."

"But —"

"And if I *ever* tell you it doesn't need to be checked, check it anyway."

Irrwaer pursed her lips. "So, you remember?"

"Dismissing you?" The Priestess nodded. "Yes. A suggestion spell, I'm certain. I failed and gave her the opening."

"You know who — ?"

"Shh."

Irrwaer quieted and focused instead on gaining a new ability at her superior's behest. *Because keeping it from me only bound my wrists when I could have done something to defend us.*

If D'Shea never reappeared, she might be in a competition with half the Sanctuary to take over for Juliran earlier rather than later. Irrwaer considered what she'd be willing to do to defend her intended place while, for added practice, she adjusted her rounds to check on Sil and the bloodstone every other mark. The magic wasn't too draining and even got easier.

The eleventh time, the penultimate check before her Priestess meant to confess their loss to the High Priestess, Irrwaer went rigid when she heard screaming in the empty room.

No. Not empty anymore.

Clutching her panic ring, Irrwaer seized Juliran's kit and ducked into the secret passage, launching into a sprint. She skidded to a stop before the runes, pausing long enough on the outside to use them for their intended purpose.

Inside, she saw Varessa D'Shea, her belly enormous, writhing in a panic on her cot. The sorceress's white shift was stained with blood, her body almost certainly in the throes of her labor.

Spider shit!

Irrwaer drew a dagger from her belt and dipped the tip in a jar from the kit before unlatching and sliding open the panel, both relieved and terrified that whoever had used the hidden door last didn't disable it.

Whoever you are, I know you wanted me to find her like this.

The acolyte drew in a deep breath, prepared to stab the first thing to reveal itself by scent, sound, or sight. She spoke the command word to light the glowstone high on the ceiling, revealing the struggles in full color.

"Get back!" D'Shea screamed, throwing an arm to cover her eyes. "S-stay away, or I'll kill you!"

The healer believed her. The sorceress's bare hands were free but bearing recent marks of restraint. A moment later, however, it became obvious she hadn't the strength to stand off the padded cot.

"Lead Sister, it's Irrwaer. Listen, I can ease the pain."

"Liar!" she snarled, her pink-stained teeth. "Shove your head back in Braqth's cunt and get out!"

Irrwaer double-checked that the sound-proof wards on the inside were undamaged. *Good.* Then she heard familiar footsteps behind her.

Thank Goddess. But why is she bringing him to see this?

"Irrwaer," Juliran said with relief, extending her arm through the doorway. "The calming aura, the three of us. Now."

"Yes, Priestess."

The acolyte grasped the offered hand, and a familiar, guided sensation arose as their magic threaded together to make their suggestion more potent to all within the room. This was the only option they had to make the patient manageable without harming the baby.

Assuming it isn't already dead from whatever happened to her.

As their auras expanded to encourage peace and quiet within the cell, the Priestess and her acolyte stepped closer to the sorceress. Each noted the obvious signs of the pregnant mata having been denied water and Reverie for too long, of familiar leather marks on her wrists and ankles, and three dark spots of spreading blood indicating probable puncture wounds.

D'Shea shook, struggled to keep her eyes on them or even to scream again. The sorceress had lost all her strength when their three auras extinguished her rage. Finally, she collapsed on her back and groaned, trying but failing to roll over. Irrwaer noticed her dark nipples leaking a yellowish-white fluid through her shift, and that there were multiple, similar stains from before which were now dried.

"Sit behind and support her back, Irrwaer. Help her breathe."

"Yes, Pr—"

"Shh. While we're here, call me Juliran or nothing at all."

Irrwaer bit her lower lip and set her dagger beneath the cot before hooking D'Shea by her armpits. Juliran kept the cot stable as Irrwaer heaved to sit their laboring patient up, before sitting behind and supporting her back.

Juliran touched the straining belly with knowledgeable hands before turning her head to press one ear and listen in on the womb in distress. Her eyes slid shut and she murmured the beginning of a chant. Irrwaer took the initiative to cover the lethargic sorceress's ears through the initial prayer, then kept watch as D'Shea's head lolled against her shoulder.

She was aware of Sil's aura helping them still to keep the peace, though his eyes were wide as he stared at the blood on white fabric.

"What?" she whispered.

His worried gaze turned to her, and he signed rather than spoke. *There's someone under there.*

Irrwaer scoffed. *Of course. She's pregnant. She will push an infant out of her body when she's regained enough strength.*

Sil shrugged, abashed. *Sorry, Acolyte.*

They sat in stillness, waiting for Juliran to finish her muttering trance, when something occurred to Irrwaer.

★Wait, Sil," she signed. ★You said 'someone'? Why? You've seen round bellies before.★

Sil shook his head, swallowing. ★Not like this. I see one … separate. From hers.★

Meanwhile, she hadn't focused on that with all the other threats around them.

★Do you see any white in the separate one?★ she signed, not quite able to adjust her eyes without risking D'Shea's calm and Juliran's concentration. ★Or anything that looks tarnished? Like it's fading, or like small voids opening up?★

The bua studied the bulge again. ★There's white. A little fading, no voids.★

The baby was still alive but not without harm.

Just then, Juliran opened her eyes with a sigh of relief and a subtle surge of her own aura. "Sil."

He turned his head. "Mother?"

"Go retrieve water from our rooms. She needs to drink."

He pushed himself up. "Yes, Mother."

Only after the bua left did Juliran reveal a bottle of water from her own pack to bring to the sorceress's parched lips. Irrwaer smirked.

"We can salvage this," the Priestess whispered. "We'll need to give her as much of *our* strength as we can without losing consciousness. The baby doesn't have much time but added magic will help."

Good to have a second opinion.

The limp, delirious mata drank with increasing desperation, her bruised eyes fluttering as if trying to open. Irrwaer met her mentor's intense gaze and nodded.

"I'm ready."

IT WAS DURING THIS BIRTH THAT IRRWAER COULD FINALLY IMAGINE WHAT MIGHT LIE in store for her. Deluges of pain wracked the Red Sister's aura, unrelated to the hard-clenching womb or the relentless stretching of flesh. It consumed so much of their collective efforts that it felt like trying to get a river to change course by burrowing new tunnels in the rock. Nothing so stubborn originated in the flesh or the aura born with it.

This lingers from contact with the Abyss.

The three stab wounds on her body.

D'Shea whimpered in ways she would have been mortified to have witnesses. Her body tremors were almost constant, as were the tears streaming down her cheeks. Neither of the healers commented, taking not a sliver of enjoyment in teetering on the precipice of failure.

We don't know who will survive this chaos flooding our infirmary.

For now, the Sanctuary servants gave of themselves to the Red Sister who needed it, the three of them working to push the clinging stink of a powerful ritual aside long enough to bring out the child they'd tended and nurtured and waited for.

Sil had returned with the water, of course, and had understood it wasn't needed at that moment. He set it aside. The females could barely acknowledge him in their attempts to keep the contractions growing or to prevent D'Shea from falling unconscious. The pretty bua sat quietly beside them, an extra set of eyes should anyone disturb them.

After almost three marks of assistance, all their endurances were beginning to flag. The room was hot and humid, filled with the breaths of panting caits and matas, humming with their magic.

"I can't," the sorceress wept. "Please … go away … let me be …"

"You cannot stop here," Juliran told her, scolding. "This is halfway upon your cliff, Varessa. You sleep, you die."

"Let me … *go*…" She shuddered. "G-Goddess, how I h-*hate* you all …"

Irrwaer heard something and opened her eyes to see Sil crawl closer. Without permission, he put both his hands on the swollen mound in front of him. Immediately, the females felt cooled, soothed. *Revived.*

Their circle fraying, now mended.

"Ta'suil!" Juliran gasped with surprise.

"He can't breathe, Mother," he said, almost begging. "How do I help him?"

D'Shea's distant stare had snapped into focus, now settling on Juliran's son. "H-how did you know?"

Irrwaer's eyebrows crawled up her sweating forehead.

So, it's a bua, not a cait.

And the sorceress had probably known for a while but said nothing.

Damn.

"Sit back, my son," Juliran commanded, discomfited by a Red Sister staring at her son. "You've already helped. We will take care of this from here."

With a glance at the moving mound beneath his fingers, Sil shifted back onto the floor, wrapping his arms around his knees as the more alert Lead Sister shifted up and finally focused her breath.

"Alright," she huffed. "Get it done."

She prepared to push and expel her son from her womb.

Finally.

For the first time since D'Shea's restless sleep had begun cycles ago, their work on the fifth floor of the Sanctuary carried on as expected. The birth entered its final stage much like the commoners back home: the mother strained, and the wet, white head crowned and black ears popped up from being bent. The Priestess stretched the birth canal gently but constantly, helping to release the head and tug the shoulders free.

Lastly, the sorceress reached deep for her final push and cried in a long wail as Juliran pulled the slimy babe, helping it slip free of his mother's body and catching him before he could roll off the cot. She moved immediately to peel off the broken sac from his face, clear his nose and mouth, and wipe him dry of all that mucus.

Definitely another bua.

When was the last time Irrwaer had seen a daughter born?

Not since I moved here.

And it seemed certain she would attempt to bear a son as well.

So strange, the seeming patterns within these walls.

Everyone had just caught their breath. Juliran cradled the infant, smiling with relief as she put her ear toward his quiet, normal breath. The danger had finally passed as death withdrew from the birthing room.

"He's well," she announced. "Do you wish to feed him?"

None of them anticipated what happened next. D'Shea looked at her son and violently jerked away from the proffered bundle, the back of her head hitting Irrwaer in the nose and the force of her revulsion pushing both of them off the cot and onto the floor.

"G-ge — !" the sorceress stuttered, choking on something as she clutched her throat, her eyes impossibly wide.

Juliran was alarmed. "D'Shea!"

Their patient twisted abruptly and vomited bile from her abused body and onto the floor. The new mata cried hoarsely, a sound raggedly pinned to a more sustained agony from before her baby was born.

"Get h-him … a … *away!*" D'Shea forced out, her tone deafening and irreconcilable. "Out! Out! *Out!*"

Juliran rose to her feet and shoved the newborn into Irrwaer's arms, who clutched for the right hold. "Take them away, both of them. Wait for me."

Once she had the baby secure in one arm, the acolyte reached for a terrified Sil's wrist, prepared to drag him if he didn't keep up. She felt the bua get his legs underneath him and hurry alongside her, and she breathed out through her nose as she once again did as she was bid.

What in the fucking web is going on?

ONE SILENT, TENSE WAIT LATER, JULIRAN JOINED THEM IN HER CHAMBERS TO RETRIEVE the baby.

"I think I have her calmed down," she said, disappearing back inside the passage. "Wait here."

After a bit longer, but too soon for a feeding, the Priestess came back with a fretting infant, a baffled look, and a shake of her head, her mouth so tight her neck raised lines.

"What is going on?" Irrwaer asked, glad that Sil had decided to hide in his room.

"She can't speak where she's been the last two cycles," Juliran said. "Which I expected. But what I didn't is … she falls into seizure if she holds her child. I … I think it could become lethal if allowed to continue."

Irrwaer had no reply, only a deep, foreboding concern for the power required for a mage to cast that strong of a geas. *She cannot hold her son … she can't feed him.*

"So," she began, "do I summon Kelfa or Beti from the nursery to feed him?"

"I will do it," Juliran said as the baby in her arms began to cry aloud. "You gather everything we would need to tend a child here until I can sort out where we stand."

"Yes, Priestess."

Irrwaer moved with welcomed familiarity about her floor, searching for the right supplies, wrestling with the unwelcome certainty that the ill-timed surprises would continue one after the other.

That feeling seemed justified when Jaunda spoke in her ear.

Hey. Where are you?

She palmed her face. *Damn it. I don't have time to fuck right now!*

Nonetheless, she went to find the Corpora.

Or let the Corpora find her.

Don't touch me! she signed with all the force she could when Jaunda cornered her in an alcove. *Your Lead just gave birth, but there are problems!*

The moderate humor glimpsed in the fighter's face wiped clean a moment later. *What problems? Is she alive?*

She lives. Greatly weakened.

The baby?

Irrwaer nodded, wondering where the lump in her throat came from. *He's alive. Hungry. She can't feed him … *

Her hands shook before Jaunda's sober eyes.

Take me to her. I need to see D'Shea.

Thankfully, they were going to skip the rut.

Without protest, Irrwaer led Jaunda through the secret passage from another entry, but when they reached the communication panel, instead of taking off her gloves, the Red Sister kicked at the stone with the toe of her boot.

"Open it up," Jaunda said. "Not using the runes this time. Let me in."

Fuuuck. I'm in so much trouble.

In truth, they were all in trouble, no matter whose other unseen fingers were stirring this pot. It only took another instant for Irrwaer to come up with her explanation, that this was not an unreasonable decision for the second healer for the infirmary to make.

Irrwaer bit her lip. *They might not expect it, would they?*

She couldn't see any of the other guards or acolytes being so concerned for her Priestess as Jaunda seemed for D'Shea.

Not unless they were failing in their orders and feared execution.

That fear did not exist in the Red Sister standing next to her.

With a soft exhale, the acolyte opened the door to the cell once again, and Jaunda surged through the moment her chest would fit. The sorceress shrieked at the sudden arrival, spinning on her cot, her bloodied shift twisted around her dark legs.

Jaunda's jaw made a grinding sound when she noted the marks of restraint and the shrunken stomach. Haunted eyes stared at them as silence fell. D'Shea clearly didn't believe the Corpora was truly there.

"Lead D'Shea?" The warrior approached slowly, taking to one knee in front of her, touching her fist to her red armor. "I'm here for my next task."

The sorceress kept staring, though she leaned forward and sniffed, seeming to recognize the scent. "Jaunda."

"Yeah. What do I do next, Lead?"

The question nearly overwhelmed as D'Shea tried to focus everywhere at once. Then her voice rasped, "Get me out."

"On it."

"What?!" Irrwaer blurted. "You can't!"

"Fucking *can*, fucking will," Jaunda said, standing up while offering a hand to her Lead. "You have your live baby. That's the only reason she was here, right?"

"You don't have her uniform," the acolyte pointed out.

The Corpora winked. "Let us worry about that."

Maddening.

"The High Priestess needs to know —"

The warrior tilted her head back and laughed, holding steady as D'Shea found her balance using her shoulder. "Fuck your 'High' Priestess."

Irrwaer flinched. "I'm not repeating that."

"As you wish. She can find out later."

"Wait, don't! Let me get Juliran."

"No!" D'Shea barked.

"But I'm fucked if you walk out!"

"I don't see why," Jaunda sneered. "Bargain's done, right?"

D'Shea slapped the Corpora's shoulder. "Get. Me. Out."

"Right."

Jaunda lifted the sorceress's arm with surprising care, drawing it across her shoulders, and looked at the acolyte. "Close the door behind us, will you, sweetmeat?" She tossed her chin toward the hall door. "And go out that way instead."

Irrwaer watched them leave and did not try to stop them. The swell of worry remained, but she closed the alternate passage and let herself out of the more complicated hallway door instead, leaving the cell wide open as she hurried back to her Priestess's quarters.

It needs purification before we use it again.

CHAPTER 8

HIGH PRIESTESS ROSHEN FINALLY STEPPED OUTSIDE OF HER EIGHTH LEVEL CHAMBERS after Irrwaer had been waiting with Juliran for over a mark among darkly vibrant decorations. The acolyte forced her toes to stop pressing the carpet.

"There you are," she said, her frown unchanging, her blonde-streaked hair piled on her head. "Come in now."

Irrwaer followed her Priestess, who was holding the new bua close to her neck as he slept. She'd given him a mild tonic in his milk to help keep him quiet for this meeting, but the apprentice wasn't sure if it would last with the time wasted so far. She had another in her bag if needed.

Roshen briefly studied the baby's face then sat at her desk, which was partly covered in scrolls and statues. A large spider web tapestry hung on the wall protecting her back. Juliran and her apprentice took the two plain seats before her, their soft shoes never contacting bare stone.

"So," their superior began. "A new bua to add to the nursery?"

"Yes, High Priestess," said Juliran, moving in a subtle rock for the baby's benefit, "until he's old enough for the Wizard's Tower."

"Hmph." The High Priestess made a face. "A disappointment. Seems we have too many males. If D'Shea had to stomp out of here after dropping the infant and insulting us the way she did, she could have at least given us a cait of that bloodline." She paused as if to ponder then hissed to herself. "I suppose his sire will find a use for him."

Juliran opted for an elegant bow of her head over a verbal response, and Irrwaer kept still with her eyes on the ground.

"How went the birth?" Roshen asked in a tone suggesting she expected an untroublesome answer.

"Strenuous and with clear resentment for her confinement," Juliran answered. "She bled more than typical. We needed to use magic to assure a live birth."

Roshen huffed. "Her fault she got pregnant under the Prime. What did she expect to have happened?" The High Priestess paused. "Maybe she thought the Headmaster couldn't spawn anymore, though the proof that she rode him so much still baffles me."

Juliran shrugged. "Phaelous is favored by the Queen still, even if he doesn't serve as a consort anymore."

The High Priestess cocked a brow and spoke dryly. "I know. But fucking him wouldn't raise Varessa's status on account of that. I haven't any idea what she planned by seducing him if it wasn't to catch a mage-child. Did she give you any hints, Juliran?"

"No, High Priestess."

"What about you, acolyte?"

Damn.

Irrwaer shook her head. "No, High Priestess. She shared nothing about the Headmaster."

"Nothing? In all her time filling a waste pot for you to empty? Impressive. Perhaps she was more smitten by him than I realized, if she risked that and simply didn't like the consequences."

Sigh.

How long would Roshen sit and talk to herself before asking for her report? Sil was waiting alone, apart from the children on the third floor. The entire infirmary was waiting as well, yet the High Priestess had summoned both healers at once.

"I heard that Corpora came back a few times as well," the High Priestess continued, causing Irrwaer's stomach to freeze.

"Under orders," Juliran replied, dark fingers lightly brushing the fine, white hair on the infant. "Are you surprised?"

"Of course not. Understand anything spoken between them?"

"No, but we wrote it down nonetheless."

"Give it to me."

Juliran nodded at Irrwaer, who stood up and brought out two pages of notes. Roshen took them, scanned with her eyes, and heaved a breath of irritation. "Hmph. Oddly uneventful clash with the Sisterhood."

Juliran shrugged. "They knew we won when D'Shea first stepped into the cell, High Priestess. Now she's just biding time."

"Hm. So be it. Add the bua to the nursery, Juliran. Usual regimen unless we hear otherwise from the Valsharess."

"Of course, High Priestess."

"Dismissed."

Irrwaer was frowning as soon as they were out of that oppressive office and taking the nearest stairwell coiling down to the fifth floor.

Waste. She didn't bother to ask any questions. Not even his name.

All the same, her Priestess had warned her only to answer the direct questions and not offer details.

"And if she pursues details, let me handle it."

Did the High Priestess *truly* believe what had happened was not a single spider's thread more complicated than they'd claimed? Or did she already know much more and merely noted how much the two healers *didn't* say?

Don't assume the latter until you have proof, Irrwaer …

Even though, usually, it was too late to back up when that proof reared its head, as it was with Wilsira waiting for them beside the door panel leading to the fifth floor. Juliran gasped, the baby squeaked softly, and Irrwaer bit her tongue.

Fuck!!

In the dim, blue glow of the stairwell, the Conceiver smiled up at them with a hint of teeth showing and a twinkle in her eyes. With calm deliberation, she placed her palm on the door which would give them escape. Both the other females could sense the spell in place.

"How did it go, Juliran?" asked Wilsira.

"Well," the Priestess answered. "A normal birth with blood, and only a new nursery addition and speculations afterward."

"I'm glad to hear it." Wilsira's gaze dropped a little. "Did she name him?"

"Uh, y-yes."

"Oh?" The Conceiver blinked then narrowed her eyes. "What name did she choose?"

Juliran blew out a breath as the baby in her arms began to fuss. "Shyntre."

"Hm. A good bua's name. When was this?"

"We received a message the next eve," Juliran answered.

"Interesting." Wilsira stepped forward and lifted her arms. "May I?"

Irrwaer tried to take a step back out of their way and then felt a hot breath on her neck. A quiet rumble sounded in the tight passage. Although Juliran kept her back to the threat, Shyntre opened his mouth and started crying while Wilsira held out her hands to take him.

"Will you give the baby back to me?" Juliran asked outright, her back rigid.

Meanwhile, the acolyte watched sickly yellow eyes appear before the rest of the white-maned demonblood.

"Of course," Wilsira answered with a smile. "I only want a closer look at our new bua."

The Priestess-healer passed D'Shea's son to the Conceiver, and Shyntre's cry turned into a wail loud enough that Irrwaer covered her ears. A moment later, she realized his wrap needed to be changed as drops of urine slid down his short, chubby legs and dripped off his toes onto the bare stairs. Wilsira wrinkled one nostril as she held him out and up, watching his head hang without support as she studied his face.

The Sathoet filling the stairwell behind them drew in a long breath, exhaling the name in a long hiss through sharp teeth which sounded like a threat. "*Shhhintreee ...*"

"Patience, Kerse," she cooed. "We're not keeping a baby. Juliran will tend him and the Consort for later."

The flash of protective anger which appeared on Juliran's face was regrettable but telling. Wilsira noticed as Irrwaer did, and the Conceiver chuckled.

"You *do* know you can't keep him forever, right, Juliran?" she teased. "Our Royal Consorts are not like our Sathoet Sons. They serve a vastly different purpose."

"And what purpose did this one serve?" the Priestess-healer asked through a tight throat, indicating the miserable child in the Conceiver's clutches.

Wilsira shifted that cunning gaze again and winked at Irrwaer. "I am sure we'll both find out."

What?

"Here, he's filthy," she finished, handing the bua back to Juliran, who immediately passed him to Irrwaer.

Sigh.

The acolyte gathered him close without concern for the stains and stepped an equal distance from Kerse and Wilsira. The Sathoet watched her every moment, his hands flexing as if on the verge of launching at her with claws out.

Or at the baby he's already jealous of.

"But I am still to place my Consort, correct, Conceiver?" Juliran asked.

Wilsira tilted her head up as her eyes rolled up and came back down. "That will be my pleasure."

"But —"

"I'm sure you can find many other pleasures with him before that time. He *will* need training, after all, like the others of the fourth level." Wilsira smiled at Irrwaer, then Kerse. "Ideally, from someone who cares enough to teach him."

Juliran stopped speaking, her mouth tight and hands folded in front of her. The other Priestess looked her up and down consideringly then snapped her fingers and pointed when Kerse lifted his foot to step toward Irrwaer.

"Back up, my son," she commanded. "Three steps."

He hissed more softly this time but obeyed. Then Wilsira turned and opened the panel door out of the stairwell for them.

"It was good crossing paths with you," she said, "but we must be on our way. Praise Braqth, the Mistress of the Labyrinth, and the Chosen."

"Praise Braqth, the Mistress of the Labyrinth, and the Chosen," Juliran and Irrwaer repeated together before moving toward the door at the Conceiver's beckoning.

Once the two healers stepped out in the pale stone halls of the infirmary, the passage closed behind them. They kept walking, turning a corner before, without speaking, they hurried to check on Sil. To his mother's unconcealed relief, the pretty bua still waited for them.

While Irrwaer cleaned up D'Shea's infant and herself, the thought came to her for the first time.

Sil will need training, to learn to couple just like I did. Probably for longer.

No doubt they must start him much earlier, for he couldn't hide his face in work like she did. No one would overlook a growing beauty like him; *someone* would want him. Who would Juliran choose when the time came? Who would she trust not to abuse him?

I hope it's not me. I can't do what Jaunda did.

Yet, if it wasn't her, the infirmary was sure to become worse with many female "prospects" sniffing around. This was something they would *all* have to deal with. Irrwaer felt pity for mother and bua, and the other females wedging themselves between them. For the first time, the acolyte gave thanks to their goddess that she was born a cait in Sivaraus.

I don't want the debt Juliran has, and I don't want a 'pure' bua before testing myself on the altar.

Irrwaer thought it over many times while she worked. She always came to the same conclusion.

An ugly half-breed might be easier for someone like me to raise, everything considered.

Little Shyntre had fallen back asleep as soon as he was clean and dry, but he would be hungry soon.

And you, Red Sister's son, she thought with a frown, watching his hand clutch her finger by reflex when she poked his palm. *What in all the Deepearth brought you here in the center of the web?*

"I am sure we'll both find out," the Conceiver had said.

Chapter 9

2897 S.E. – The Sanctuary of Sivaraus

Seven turns passed.

Most of a decade, yet it seems longer.

These were quiet times compared to the one turn previous with the Red Sister in residence on the fifth floor. Varessa D'Shea never came back, and the Conceiver and her Sathoet Son had left the healers alone after trapping them in the stairwell to look at her baby.

Afterward, Juliran didn't confide what her chains with Wilsira actually were; perhaps, like D'Shea, she simply could not say. Irrwaer asked few questions because it was obvious to her that the Conceiver plotted against the High Priestess. Somehow, the Red Sister sorceress and her child had been ensnared into the long game.

Roshen doesn't seem to have the imagination Wilsira does.

Did the acolyte see any benefit in giving her superior the warning that Juliran couldn't?

None. There is only punishment for us both.

Irrwaer had her hands full tending a new child anyway, one whom the Priestesses had aggressively claimed from the Sisterhood yet had no immediate plans for because of his sex. No one seemed concerned or curious about Shyntre, so Irrwaer filled the void of neglect as part of her duties, taking him with her as she worked.

"You *could* leave him with the wet nurses on the third floor, Irrwaer," Juliran pointed out once. "Rather than returning for him each time."

The acolyte shrugged, glancing at Sil, who smiled at her for some reason. "Hm. I've noticed I get less trouble from patients and acolytes when I have the bua on my back than when I don't."

Tiredly, her Priestess sighed and nodded. "Very well. I suppose it does please the Queen that every cait helps assure the survival of new infants. We need them so badly. Continue as you wish."

The acolyte did so while fully aware she merely waited for the next scheme in which she or Shyntre could become a puppet or a hostage. It wasn't as if either of them had any power or anyone to truly protect them, not even Juliran. Irrwaer doubted the stern claims that every live birth was so precious to the levels above; surely, nothing beyond usefulness as workers.

Some babies are more precious than others. You and I have more in common with each other than not, little bua.

The acolyte would never forget when the first Worship Ball happened. At first, she was taken aback by the intense preparation and the excitement throughout the Palace-Sanctuary complex. She was sometimes rolled over by the flurries of questions about how one could guarantee "grabbing one."

They mean a Royal Consort. As if I would know?

The first generation of pureblood Priestess sons had come of age on the fourth floor mostly out of Irrwaer's sight. She had never felt curiosity to explore the floor in between the Matron-less youths on the third and the injured or ill on the fifth. She'd been forbidden regardless.

There were only eight mature Consorts to be presented at the Worship Ball in front of Matrons and representatives from more than twenty Houses of Sivaraus. In the seventeen cycles since Irrwaer had arrived at the Sanctuary, these hidden sons had been trained to please the Nobles in their bedchambers, to serve the Matron obediently, and to help quicken multiple wombs on each plantation.

Supposedly, these sons were coveted because they were all mageborn, if untrained, and the Priestess's bloodlines would boost the magical potential of the favored Houses to whom they were gifted.

The competition would be intense.

No wonder it's Wilsira's pleasure to place them all.

"Stay in my chamber with both buas while I'm at the Ball," Juliran instructed as she prepared for the ceremonies. "Do not leave them for *any* reason."

"Yes, my Priestess."

More of the same, and not a bad thing.

She was mildly curious if the Royal Consorts were as beautiful as others claimed, but Juliran had explained that each would have to prove his ability to perform upon the altar, in front of all their guests, and that his cream was fertile before the House would accept him.

"Sounds like a long eve," Irrwaer said with cautious humor.

Juliran's eyes flicked briefly to her, then to Sil, who was helping her layer her gown just right. "Agreed. I hope it might at least prove … instructive."

Her own attentive bua kept his eyes on the ground and played his usual pretty-and-dumb act, but Irrwaer was certain he knew Juliran's determination to attend had everything to do with him.

He's almost fifty.

If she was lucky, they had two more decades before he would be on the altar before the Matrons. If the Conceiver didn't step in earlier to have him "educated."

Sil grew moodier after his mother left for the Ball but didn't speak what was on his mind. He was talking less in general, which was normal for his age. Nonetheless, he found ways of increasing her own annoyance as they were each confined to their Priestess's chambers with a toddler who had recently passed from urgent crawling to an astonishingly confident walk. Shortly before that eve, Irrwaer had discovered the bua could run if he wanted and choose to evade her.

He was becoming more difficult to catch.

"Shyntre!" she exclaimed, tugging him out of the third basket he'd located beneath a standing chest and started digging through it. "You don't know what's dangerous in there!"

"Lemme go!" he demanded.

"He doesn't care," Sil remarked alongside the child's growling protest.

Irrwaer wrenched the bua's hands free and placed the basket far above his head as he whined in frustration. "He *should* care if he knows what's good for him!"

The older youth reclined on the side bed, weaving fine, multi-colored threads into a bracelet as the younger bua grew even more stubborn and restless. "So, why aren't you calming his aura like usual, Acolyte?"

Because the bua's been learning to resist that, and he gets worse than this.

Sil smiled at her silence, almost as if he knew the answer to his own question. Irrwaer scowled back at him, lips pursed tight.

"I am curious, Acolyte," said Juliran's son. "Why do you not strike him to teach him where not to go in Mother's rooms? Others have insisted it works."

Irrwaer had only tried that once.

Once.

"Because it damages my healing magic somehow," she told him, drawing his attention sharply. "It hurts me."

The youth blinked and sat up. "Wh ... what?"

"Yeah," the acolyte sneered. "Have you ever wondered why Juliran has never struck you? Have *you* ever felt the impulse to hit Shyntre, no matter how much he cries?"

Sil's very pretty set of eyes widened in what appeared to be a genuine revelation. Irrwaer snorted, shaking her head in contempt.

"We must be the only three Davrin in the whole Sanctuary whose magic suffers for disciplining a child," she said, crossing her arms, looking to one side before rushing after the bua when he'd vanished into the next room.

So wearisome.

But she couldn't let the child throw all Juliran's things everywhere, so she was stuck chasing him around until she returned.

"Where is he?!" she cried after coming back empty-handed to the sitting room.

The future consort was trying not to laugh. He pointed at the walk-in wardrobe, its large door ajar revealing numerous robes and gowns.

"Shyntre! Get out of there!"

Irrwaer ducked her head in and paused, momentarily stunned to see the way to the secret passage open.

I don't believe this.

"He's in the walls," she barked. "Stay here, Sil!"

"I will, Acolyte."

He will, Irrwaer knew as she left Juliran's quarters, *because he knows what's good for him. When Juliran comes back, maybe it's time to talk about putting Shyntre permanently on the third floor with the rest. I can't discipline him like he needs, but the others there can.*

A Red Sister's son couldn't be permitted to run wild like this!

Irrwaer caught up to the bua standing still, his hands flat upon the panel which led into the solitary room where he'd been born. The acolyte froze in place, overtaken by some nameless fear.

How did he know? Was he drawn here, somehow?

Then she realized that the magic shouldn't be working for him. That cell was supposed to be empty. They hadn't checked the bloodstone in spans. *There was no reason to.*

"Shyntre?" she whispered as he stared at the stone.

He didn't hear her.

There's someone in there.

She reached out and squeezed his small shoulder. "Shyntre?"

"Hm?"

"What do you see in there?"

Irrwaer watched his expression shift through befuddlement to worry to sadness.

"Gold eyes," he said.

Kerse.

Had Wilsira come for one of their buas at last? Had the Conceiver sent her Sathoet Son to lure D'Shea's son away from them while his Priestess was busy at the Worship Ball?

"Here, let me see."

Irrwaer reached for his wrists, wrapping her aura protectively around his as she tugged his hands gently away. Shyntre winced when contact broke, blinking rapidly, but he allowed her to put his arms around her waist instead. He held on tight while she placed her hands on the panel to see inside the cell.

Her middle went cold to see an emaciated male with solid gold hair and eyes, wearing only a waist wrap, his dark skin dry and bearing old scars. *Not*

Kerse.

Unless it was an illusion?

Headmaster Phaelous?

No, he was too short. *And* too young.

Who is this? How did his eyes shine like jewelry?

Irrwaer gasped when she realized he wasn't just looking at the wall. The prisoner was focused on her, *looking* at her.

He lifted a thin hand and signed with an odd flair.

★Come in. Both of you.★

Oh, Goddess.

She couldn't move. The ancient blond saw it. He licked his cracked lips and signed again.

★Please. I beg you.★

The acolyte would never understand why she broke at once, why her hands opened the secret door, but they did. Shyntre stepped in first, looking around though more wary than before. Irrwaer followed, seizing hold of his small hand to keep him next to her. She could hear her heart in her ears, which meant they heard it, too.

The unknown prisoner in D'Shea's old cell smiled at her, a view she had never glimpsed in her life. She was struck by a soft emotion without a name woven with another one which brightened his eyes a bit, though both of them darkened with regret.

Then his head drooped like he hadn't the strength to keep it up for long. Irrwaer realized he was looking at Shyntre, who stared back at him. Tears arose and escaped those impossibly metallic Davrin eyes.

His lips shaped words without voice: *I'm sorry.*

"W-who are you?" she forced out, squeezing her bua's hand hard enough that he whined. "How did you get in here?"

The blond stranger's eyes dropped from the child to his own lap, and he said nothing. He went still as if waiting for something inevitable.

Then she heard footsteps behind her.

"Conceiver?" Irrwaer called out, turning her back away from the open passageway and dragging Shyntre with her. She aimed for the front door leading into the hallway, reaching to start the sequence to open it. "Is it you?"

Someone laughed softly in the darkness.

Then *She* stepped out.

"No, child. We are not Wilsira."

Irrwaer nearly fainted meeting that tawny gaze the first time. She collapsed onto her hands and knees, just holding consciousness as her head swam. In her fall, she'd released her bua and wasn't sure if he was still there. Blindly, she patted the bare floor nearby.

"Shyntre?"

"He is safe with Us."

Not true.

Not from the way Shyntre called her name, his small, bare feet kicking something soft and fine as he sought to escape their Queen.

"Irrwaer!"

"Calm down," she cried helplessly, blinking as she fought to clear her sight. "Calm, please, don't hit —"

His crying grew closer to her, yet quieter.

Until it stopped.

Then a hard hand took her by the arm, pulling her to her feet. The acolyte's nose was briefly overwhelmed with fragrances of incense rising from the fine, velvety cloth of royal purple and gold. Small fingers scraped her shoulder as her young charge just missed catching her robe before falling asleep in royal arms.

In the silence which followed, Irrwaer dared not look up from the waist of the gown again.

"We remember this one," She said, twisting her neck toward the malnourished male on the cot. "You attempted to hide Our vision."

"We are ... sorry to disturb you," he whispered.

"Only because you were caught."

The ancient fingers dug harder into the acolyte's muscle as Her irritation bled into the Queen's voice, and Irrwaer bit her cheek so hard her eyes blurred with tears.

What is happening?

The Queen's neck twisted around again. "Acolyte. Look at Us."

No ...

Irrwaer struggled with the same urge to piss herself as when the Driders had appeared on the dock, but she obeyed. She looked.

The eyes of the Valsharess were like translucent topaz, staring in the distance. Her hair was long, solid gold, and plaited from the elegant crown of woven silver threads down to the floor. Her face held more centuries and age creases than any Dark Elf she'd seen up close, but they hardly moved when She spoke.

"Do you wish to become a full Daughter of Braqth, Acolyte?"

"Y-yes, Valsharess," Irrwaer answered, unable to stop her shaking. "Some … decade, perhaps."

"How long have you been training in the Sanctuary?"

Blood pumped through her chest, causing a throbbing in her ears.

"Uh … a-almost two decades?"

The Valsharess released her arm. "That is enough for one like you."

Irrwaer just caught herself from another fall. She touched her arm.

The tips of my fingers are numb.

"The High Priestess shall summon you within three cycles of the Worship Ball's end," She continued. "Be ready to become who you are."

What?

Three cycles.

Abruptly, the hall door opened, and Irrwaer jumped back as the Queen approached it, carrying D'Shea's son as he slept. The Valsharess extended Her arm, beckoning, and the golden-eyed bua dragged himself off the cot, gripping the edge to assure his precarious balance on scarred, bare feet.

"Return to your chambers, Irrwaer," She said as her hand rested lightly on the old bua's peeling back. "You may not speak of this."

Finally, the two of them stepped out into the hall.

They took Shyntre with them.

No.

And the door closed on its own.

Locked.

Irrwaer turned and ran back into the passage. Her hands quaked with every motion to secure her path behind her. When she finally stumbled back into Juliran's wardrobe, having felt lost in a labyrinth for marks, Sil was there to meet her.

"There you are! Where is Shyntre? Did you find him?"

He sounded worried.

"Sh-She *took* him —" the acolyte began, clutching her gut as the pain started.

"Who took him? The Conceiver?"

No!

Irrwaer wailed in the wake of sudden, intense grief.

"Acolyte?!"

"My bua … ! My bua, I-I won't s-see him again! I … I didn't know … I didn't mean … c-cannot think …"

She wanted to fall over dead. Helplessly, Sil opened his arms in a silent offering, and for the first time since they met, Irrwaer accepted.

The acolyte collapsed against the youth, and the fellow healer held on while she wept for this fresh, unfamiliar wound.

She mourned until their Priestess returned from the Ball.

IRRWAER HAD NO CHOICE BUT TO BE SILENT ON THE TOPIC OF D'SHEA'S SON VANISH-ing while Juliran was gone. Fortunately, her Priestess seemed to understand. If it was indeed the Conceiver, as she'd pressed, the Priestess-healer would find out sooner or later.

Unfortunately, the following summons from Roshen the next cycle caught her entirely off guard.

"What?!" Juliran screeched as they once again stood inside her own chambers. "She undergoes her trials now?!"

"Watch your tone!" barked the High Priestess. "You heard me. Prepare Acolyte Irrwaer for the altar. You have two cycles."

After Roshen left, Irrwaer smiled wanly, and Juliran blinked.

"You knew," her elder murmured.

She couldn't even nod her head to confirm.

I'm sorry.

CHAPTER 10

EIGHT RED SISTERS STOOD GUARD INSIDE THE RITUAL CHAMBER AS CLUSTERS OF young, intoxicated Nobles entered from the Palace and stumbled about the floor.

One of the guards was familiar.

Under the pretense of helping to light the heatless torches, Irrwaer stepped closer to the elite in red leather who stood nearest to the platform stairs. When the acolyte peered a little harder, the Red Sister turned her head, and a familiar face smirked before winking at her.

Irrwaer couldn't believe her eyes.

Corpora Jaunda was present at her trial.

She's going to witness me fail or succeed.

But of course, she would want to watch. Perhaps it was a good sign that a new candidate for Priestess felt her middle tremble in some way other than fear.

Would that she could prepare me —

Then the idea struck.

"Priestess Juliran," Irrwaer said as she approached.

Her mentor was one of three Priestesses chosen to hold the demon within the borders of the ritual if Irrwaer lost control or was killed before banishing him away. Juliran looked up from her standing table, managing to hide her

concerns about the break-neck speed of their ritual training and preparation.
"Yes?"

"You said I was allowed one method to temper tolerance to pain."

"Yes. You chose the blade."

"I've changed my mind. I'll take the whip."

"What? Are you sure?"

Irrwaer motioned toward the Red Sister closest to the altar. "And I'd like Corpora Jaunda to wield it. Either on or off the platform, whatever is more appropriate."

Juliran blinked but considered with one look at her acolyte's old body trainer then another to the two other Priestesses. Neither was the Conceiver, a result of immense effort on part of Irrwaer's mentor to persuade the High Priestess not to choose her.

"Hm, I see," the elder healer murmured. "Unusual but not forbidden. Are you sure you want everyone in the Sanctuary to know you've submitted to a Sister's Feldeu?"

Irrwaer shrugged. "Better than dying. And she can make me wetter than I can get on my own. I've tried."

Juliran was convinced, so Irrwaer let her convince the others.

THE HARD STONE OF THE ALTAR PRESSED INTO HER BARE BELLY AS THE ORGY ON THE floor gradually grew with powerful lust. Irrwaer clutched the edges without restraints or clothing, her naked ass already burning as Jaunda exchanged her gloved hand for a real whip handed to her in proper ceremony by Juliran.

"Having fun, sweetmeat?" the Corpora murmured when she leaned down, a heavy hand pressed to her back, and nipped her ear.

"The *best* of times," Irrwaer replied in a dry taunt.

"Heh. Odd cait."

The whip was a first between them, but her gut had been right about the Red Sister knowing how to use it. Despite the massive difference between her palm and those lashes, somehow the confident cock-wielder would have

the Priestess-to-be crying for leniency without a drop of blood being spilt.

"Alright, alright. Just one more."

Crack!

"Goddess!!" Irrwaer screamed full-throated above the moaning and wailing of the piles of Nobles.

"By the Pit, that ass is beautiful ..."

Jaunda sounded out of breath as she spoke, stepping up close behind the acolyte and taking hold of her hips. Irrwaer once again felt those hard thighs against the backs of her legs then the firm prod of a slicked-up phallus against her pucker. Her body relaxed immediately to let her in.

"Open wide," Jaunda said.

Irrwaer's head jerked up from the altar, her mouth open without sound as Jaunda leaned in, penetrating full-length on the first stroke almost without friction.

It felt ... good?

How?

She smeared something on it.

And Irrwaer's back hole was starting to tingle.

Oh, Goddess ...

The Red Sister knew she didn't have long before she would be escorted off the platform; she also knew Irrwaer was better off with a bit more pain to prepare her for what was coming. Jaunda fucked her hard and quick, intent on reaching her climax without slowing.

Irrwaer just held on. *Yes. Ungh! Keep going ...*

The Corpora reached her peak just in time, her growl of release somehow causing the whole room to moan. Irrwaer grunted when Jaunda's hand slapped down to hold her in place. Her asshole emptied quickly but was buzzing like a thousand wizard's sparks when Jaunda leaned down again.

"Bind that mother-rutter until he can't move, Irrwaer," she whispered. "Then shave off all his spines before you grant him that silky cunt of yours."

"Enough, Corpora," said the second Priestess, Haeva. "You must leave this platform now."

Jaunda licked Irrwaer's ear, dipping a finger between her swollen netherlips to remind her how wet she was. "Whatever you pull, priestlet, don't pull it

halfway."

Priestlet. Heh.

Not for long.

The Priestesses stepped in to remove the Red Sister and begin setting the triple-protection of the circle. Juliran and Haeva aided a groggy Irrwaer to climb properly atop the altar and settle onto her back. During that laborious process, the young healer's eyes drifted over the mass of dark, writhing bodies on the floor in front of her.

Huh. They're all fucking ...

Every one of them.

Rising, collective magic filled the room with its hum, and Irrwaer fell onto her back with a sigh, oddly unafraid as they bound her to the altar with three belts across her waist. She needed her limbs free to control and couple with the beast, but she couldn't be knocked off the altar or roll onto the floor of her own accord.

Bind him.

Shave off his spines ...

Don't do it halfway.

The three Priestesses around her would summon the correct male demon from the Abyss and prevent him from escaping past the platform into the crowd. Irrwaer needed to control him long enough to take his seed and, ideally, banish him back herself. New priestesses who succeeded in sending the sire back carried more respect than those who needed help to do it.

Either way, as long as I'm alive and carrying a son ...

A child not even the Valsharess could take away.

Hazy colors coalesced above her for quite some time as she practiced her breathing, listened to the pleasure-pain in her body, and strengthened her focus and aura. Finally, something starkly bright cut once across the ceiling. Then it came again, and a tiny gate of the Void opened up, consuming the hottest air of the hall and allowing only one body to slip through.

Suddenly, he was there.

Dropped on top of her, crushing her breath.

She felt claws in her hips. Heard an eager snarl. She recognized a hot erection dragging along her bare thigh; this one scratched her, leaving abrasions

as it sought the core of her. He drooled on her breasts. Licking them. Then *biting*.

The healer's aura flared open under those first, successive pains. She caught and held them, prepared to ride this new rush as she had Jaunda's storm of lashings.

Not passive and mewling, though.

She was ready to share the pain of their injuries *and* all her magic to heal them. Her will punched straight through the creature's aura, weakened by his arrival, then she set the hooks he would not escape while she lived.

Pain and healing in one. Not one without the other.

She would know his desires now.

They were likely much simpler than hers.

The dark, yellow-eyed demon screeched in surprise next time he bit her, and then he laughed, drawing his bristly body up almost vertical as if to finally look at her face. Irrwaer looked back, her mind aware of what she saw but more intent on gradually drawing him closer in aura and body, feeling and *knowing* the cacophony of chiming blacks and blues swirling around him like shards.

"You're in constant pain, demon," she whispered, her own nerves ablaze. "Your body ... bones always shifting ... spines breaking through your flesh —"

I liiike it! he boasted, baring sharp teeth in a wet grin. *Annd ssso will youuu ... *

"I will not. While you're here, I will take the pain away."

HA! he barked, arching his back and raking her sides. *Ahahahaha!*

His misaligned hips shifted so the pointed tip of his searing phallus prodded at her. He never blinked; he stared her down.

Take the paaain yoursssself, tasty Baenar. Take it all!

He shoved it in, spines and all, and Irrwaer saw only light behind her eyes as her arms and legs clutched him, held him in place. The budding Priestess drew on his potent magic to heal herself before repaying him with strength to spare.

The next moment, Irrwaer took his pain away.

Gradually, hers faded but for mild throbbing between her legs.

Wha — ?! The demon panicked. He tried to pull out. *Noooo!*

"Stay! Give me my son!" she yelled, gripping his black mane to keep him down. "That's why you're here!"

He felt her command through her magic's hooks; on instinct, he hunched into her then stopped. He was still erect but unsure if he knew how to cum this way. Irrwaer chuckled at this while the chanting and crying grew stronger around them.

"We have something in common?"

Onnnly becausse of youuu, he hissed. *Your rulesss. Your lawsss on thisss plane!*

Well, then.

The first rule should be obvious.

"This doesn't have to bleed, demon."

Shave off his spines.

He rumbled, trembling as she healed him further, reversing the aggressive growths on his back and around his crotch, especially those inside her, and setting the small bones in balance as she understood it. His prick may have had little bumps left but was no longer a chaotic weapon.

She moved her hips, testing as multiple high pitches vibrated in her ears. "Mm. Better. You recognize this?"

The darkest beast she'd ever witnessed glared at her, eyes so familiar in their sickly yellow pallor. *Nnno ... *

"No? This is 'pleasure,' demon. The opposite of pain. I recently learned to recognize it myself."

He tested a thrust, and Irrwaer moaned softly in the rush he felt.

Rrrrmm? Pleasssurrre ... ?

The male was so confused.

"Service me," she said through bared teeth. "Give me the grandson of our goddess. You will know the pinnacle of pleasure for it. This is our trade to honor our goddess."

The demon hesitated, drawing his prick out slowly.

It felt ... *so good.*

He pushed in again. Soft as silk.

"Do it!" she barked. "More!"

He huffed, slammed his cock into her, growled, his mane standing up on end as their skin crackled with magic. He pulled out and lunged in again with a howl to the ceiling.

"Yes!" she cried, spreading her legs wide, toes in the air.

He gave her no more cuts in rutting her, and he never stepped off the altar; he just held on. Pumping without cease. Moving with ecstasy.

When he finally roared, heralding the spurting of his seed, his burning aura mingled with hers, sharing his ultimate release with her. There were no more blood stains than there had been at the beginning.

They weren't needed.

We're healed.

For now.

Irrwaer banished him when the demonblood sire was least prepared for it, right before he rested his muzzle on her chest. Juliran began the closing chants as the others claimed complete success to the drunken, partly conscious crowd covered in their own fluids.

Amid all that noise, Irrwaer still heard Jaunda's cheer at the base of the stairs.

CHAPTER 11

2899-2965 S.E. – THE SANCTUARY OF SIVARAUS

TWO TURNS LATER, JULIRAN HELPED ASSURE THAT THEIR YOUNGEST PRIESTESS WOULD survive giving birth. There wasn't as much blood as they expected.

"You stunted him in the womb," the Priestess said with an odd contempt. "You used too much healing on him."

Irrwaer's infant Sathoet didn't have teeth or claws yet. As a result, she wasn't scarred by his birth, though she possessed scars from his sire which sometimes flared up.

"If this becomes known, you may not be considered a real Priestess, Irrwaer."

She ground her teeth. "Will you tell anyone?"

"No," Juliran answered.

That would be true for now, but not forever.

The High Priestess offered Irrwaer a suite of her own on the sixth floor while she trained and bonded with her new son. She accepted, for she could already sense the animosity from Juliran, not only from her lack of birthing scars but on behalf of her elder's growing Royal Consort.

She still can't accept she's going to lose Ta'suil to Wilsira and the Matrons. She no longer wants my help with him.

And Irrwaer didn't truly want to watch Sil's training begin anyway. She didn't want to see how it changed the sweet bua she knew, bit by bit, cycle to cycle.

After fifteen turns, she moved out of the infirmary.

I'm not used to the quiet.

Or the lack of work.

Lying in her own full bed, reflecting on this incredibly rare time of rest, Irrwaer looked down at her Sathoet after he'd finished nursing. His wasn't an Elven face at all, but one with a muzzle and a short, fuzzy stripe of white from his head all the way down his back. His ears were long and pointed, but too long, so they drooped and curled at the end.

He had a bit of a tail she was told would become less prominent with time, and his eyes were a hazy grey without pupils, though they would turn yellow once he started eating solid meat. He didn't have teeth or claws to eat that way, but she had a few plans for dealing with those traits.

Her child was so quiet most of the time; it took very little of her aura to calm him. Just a touch. It was easier than any child she'd dealt with.

I wonder how long this will last.

Perhaps as long as they had the bond.

"Is he even alive or are your sound wards that good?" Tarra asked in her open doorway, folding her arms, and arching a brow. "I haven't heard his shriek once on this floor."

With a smile, Irrwaer picked her Sathoet up and showed her new peer that her son was indeed alive. Tarra didn't study him as long as she had Sil and Shyntre.

"Hmph. How do you call him?"

"He is Vesram," Irrwaer answered.

The grey-eyed Sathoet perked up, his long, ragged ears lifting in response to her voice.

"Well, at least he recognizes it," Tarra observed. "Sometimes they aren't even that smart. I assume you have his plane-binding name?"

Irrwaer rolled her eyes. "Of course, Confessor. I knew it before he was born."

"Well, don't be stupid and lose it to someone else. That'll break your power and you might as well age a thousand turns in one cycle."

"So I've been warned."

Tarra grinned then. "I'm glad you've finally broken the threads with Juliran, you know. You might be her likely successor, but two Priestesses running the same floor is just asking for a rush of poisonings."

"Mm-hm."

"Oh! By the way, what happened to Shyntre? He was just *gone* from the fifth floor one cycle, and you used to carry him *every*where." The slightly older Priestess narrowed her eyes in thought. "Right around the time you were Chosen for the altar, wasn't it?"

Irrwaer looked behind her until the tic above her eye settled down, then looked back. "I don't know. I think Juliran placed him on the third floor, then someone moved him again. They didn't tell me where."

Tarra lifted her eyes to the ceiling. "Mm-hm. A mystery? How interesting, don't you agree? Now that you're a Priestess proper, you need to investigate these things more, Irrwaer. You're expected to if you want to climb the ranks."

"Perhaps I shall, then," Irrwaer lied, glancing up the hall from her door at the end. "Hm. Where is *your* son, Tarra?"

Her nose wrinkled. "Somewhere safe. If you're suggesting these two babies meet each other, it's not a good idea. He would tear little Vesram apart. I'm thinking of accepting the Conceiver's offer to speed his growth a little so he can be put with the others sooner."

"The Conceiver's offer?" Irrwaer repeated, frowning. "And where *are* the others?"

Tarra's smile returned, her cunning eyes flicking to the demonblood in her arms. "Oh, give it time. You'll see."

No one had been lying about how quickly the Grandson of Braqth living in her chambers would enhance her magic as he grew. Swiftly receding were the memories where it had been difficult to access her aura or the intuitive understanding of how to make her will manifest.

Incredible.

His physical growth seemed to reflect her magical strength. By his second decade, Vesram had his rows of sharp teeth and strong, vicious claws. His eyes had filled in and turned yellow. His mane grew in thick and stark white, as did the patches at his elbows, hind legs, and around his genitals. He'd also caught up in size to Tarra's son, then surpassed it, and it was no longer a question of who would tear apart who.

"What in the underground are you feeding him?" the Confessor laughed, hiding her envy and discomfort.

"Enough," Irrwaer replied with a vague smile.

Over the next half-century with her half-blood at her side, Irrwaer would expand her talents beyond direct healing, developing stable and mobile methods of mending which moved beyond the infirmary. She also attended the rituals she'd missed out on before, which gave her the opportunity to learn and relearn names far beyond her floor in the Sanctuary.

Lead D'Shea is now Elder D'Shea, just as a start.

Irrwaer had gotten a glimpse of Shyntre's mother at the next Worship Ball, which would finally separate Juliran from her pureblood son. The Red Sister didn't seem as interested in this detail as Irrwaer was.

She's watching the Matron from House Thalluen. Rohenvi.

The Matron Rohenvi already had her coveted First Daughter by the first Royal Consorts, yet she was back at Court, competing for another. Perhaps the Daughters of the Twelfth House, once dead center and stagnating in their place, might start a war to claim new lands, slaves, and resources in the next century.

Meanwhile, young Ta'suil had grown up to become a breathtaking breeding male; even Irrwaer conceded that. His long hair styled to perfection, his grace followed wherever he moved, and everything about his subservient attitude paired with physical flawlessness would have the Matrons pulling each other's earrings out to get the better look at him.

The bribery for the first ownership of his young pole had no doubt been fierce, but Wilsira ultimately placed him with the Second House, Tachna. *Her own.*

No one was surprised, but almost everyone complained.

Later that eve, after all the Consorts had been given out, Irrwaer explored more of the Palace while she was here. Walking with confidence and her Sathoet behind her, no one dared stop her.

She only stopped herself when she saw him.

"Shyntre?"

The half-grown bua whipped his head around as if he'd been caught in a trap, his crimson eyes much like his mother glinting oddly in the dim light. Vesram growled softly behind her.

"It *is* you," she said, stepping forward. "Hold a moment."

He disobeyed and sprinted away.

Fast as ever.

The Priestess pursued the bua without rancor or excess noise, aware she would likely be stopped by some obstacle.

That obstacle, as it turned out, was his sire.

"Headmaster Phaelous," she said as she approached, smiling. "What a surprise to see you here."

The elder wizard turned to smile and bowed to her with perfect Court grace and respect, allowing his son to hide behind his robes. "Priestess Irrwaer. How you've grown."

"Hmph." She scratched Vesram's chin when he growled for attention. "Have you been tutoring your son all this time?"

The tall male bowed again. "Only as I've been bid, Priestess."

As cheeky as the response was, something about the ancient male's face dissuaded her from asking specifics. Belatedly, when Shyntre peeked suspiciously out at her, she realized both sire and son possessed odd, golden flecks in their dark red irises.

For an instant she felt cold but didn't know why.

"Mothherrr?" Vesram asked.

"We'll leave soon," she reassured him.

Then Phaelous added, "Perhaps you could use added assistance on the third floor, Priestess?"

"Huh?" She swallowed as Vesram and Shyntre glared at each other. "Oh, no. Not necessary."

"What about the fourth or fifth?"

She squinted at him. "That isn't yours to decide, Headmaster."

The old wizard's age creases showed as he smiled. "Of course not, Priestess."

All the same, his generous offers urged her to leave the Palace sooner rather than later.

"THERE YOU ARE," SAID THE CONCEIVER.

She sounded in a good mood.

"Priestess Wilsira Tachnathon," Irrwaer bowed, mimicking her tone of delight.

As the elder Priestess and her Sathoet approached, her eyes moved slowly over the younger and smaller Sathoet behind Irrwaer. Kerse noticed and snarled. He was without doubt capable of tearing her bua apart.

"Enough," Wilsira commanded, slapping his face open-handed. "I'm not in the mood, Kerse."

Vesram slowly crouched behind Irrwaer, braced to protect her but posing no other challenge to the older half-blood. He kept his focus on Kerse's hands, not his eyes, and the elder Sathoet had little choice but to accept the act of submission after getting hit in the face.

Irrwaer squeezed Vesram's fuzzy shoulder, touching his aura as softly. *Good bua. I'm here.*

Her son relaxed beneath her fingers, staying silent and watchful.

"How well you've trained him, Irrwaer," said Wilsira as she caught every motion of this exchange. "I have never seen such discipline at this age. How did you accomplish it?"

I cannot hit him. I must find other ways.

Irrwaer's smile strained as she sucked in her cheeks rather than admit that to this Priestess. "We have a strong bond."

"Ah! I know what you mean."

The Conceiver chuckled, reaching to caress her son's long jaw, making him purr just moments after making him wince. He seemed hungry in more ways than one.

"I've been watching you these last fifty turns, Irrwaer, and I'm impressed. Tarra ultimately decided to enlist her Sathoet among the others in the chamber."

"I heard, Conceiver."

"Yet you don't seem to need the same refuge from their inevitable demands on our time."

"I do not, Conceiver. Not at this time."

"Hmm." Wilsira tilted her head to get a better look at the crouching youth. "Well. He might be too timid for the chamber as he is. Just as well his Mother protects him for a little longer. Though, do reach out if this changes. I have the most experience helping other matas with their Sathoets."

No doubt.

Irrwaer bowed. "Thank you, Conceiver. We are always pleased to be remembered."

Chapter 12

2965-2979 S.E. - Sivaraus

THE FIRST TIME HER BUA TOOK A SECOND WHIFF AT A SERVING CAIT AND WATCHED her for several moments too long as she hurried around a corner, Irrwaer didn't know what to do next.

Oh, no.

Vesram had been getting larger over the last twenty turns, developing more spines on his back and a new musk in his scent which reminded her of male *uroan* too distracted to pull a cart around the city. She'd responded by giving him his own room, still apart from the others on the top floor, and which sometimes needed to be locked.

With the only alternative being Wilsira, Irrwaer accepted the destruction inside, and the various messes he had to clean up later as he learned to find his own release.

He isn't the same as me in this way.

He had real urges which he *had* been governing himself for quite a while. But now he was watching the more vulnerable caits like he wanted to stalk them for meat.

Almost certainly the case, just of a different sort.

Vesram wouldn't be content with just himself locked in a room forever. How would she handle this?

Not like Wilsira and Kerse.

The Conceiver was well known for luring in endless lines of young caits to slake her son's impulses, and to be present to humiliate them as he did so. Gossip said even some of the Red Sisters had been subjected to Wilsira's games before they gained more status. Some had been mere recruits still being considered.

How do the Sathoet up on the twelfth floor find release?

Irrwaer had a few ideas based on things she'd heard or knew from the last century she'd spent in the Sanctuary. The chaos of it made her healer's aura ache just to see it in her mind's eye.

She exhaled. *Even Red Sisters know the half-bloods. Hm.*

"Lucky Priestess," Jaunda said, clapping her shoulder with a too-familiar grin. "My Elder likes this idea. You showed up and followed through. I think you're gonna gain her attention. The good kind."

Perhaps.

They stood outside a stone "cache" claimed by the Sisterhood, not far from the Sanctuary but hidden by crevices and a series of tunnels. Irrwaer hadn't known it was there until she was told where to go.

The Priestess nodded stiffly, watching the boulder move into place after Vesram had waved farewell at her. Her heart was pounding loud enough for Jaunda to hear it. "And you tell me the truth, Lead? They won't damage him if he does not harm them first?"

"I know my caits, Priestess, I picked 'em. Don't worry, they'll give him a good time. But we should stay out here and wait."

That was going to be the hardest part.

Irrwaer took a deep breath, closing her eyes briefly as she let it out. When she opened them, Jaunda was looking her up and down.

"Haven't gone off the cliff yet," she said. "Almost think your concern for raising the half-breed is keeping you sane."

Irrwaer narrowed her eyes. "His name is Vesram."

Jaunda chuckled. "Vesram. Got it."

"And what do you mean, Lead, about not going off the cliff yet?"

The warrior cocked a white eyebrow. "Not a single Priestess in the Sanctuary would reach out to the Sisterhood to teach her bua how to use his prick *and* agree, as his mata, to keep out of it. You're obviously not drinking the spider spit, or you'd be losing your shit right now."

That tremor in her middle was back.

"Every other Priestess *would* say I am insane for *wanting* this for him," she muttered.

Jaunda snorted, shrugging. "They don't get out of their pit often enough to reckon that. Just starin' at their own cunts for decades on end."

"And I'm not?"

"You just climbed out, and you hardly look at your cunt at all unless I'm there."

Irrwaer's face flushed as she jerked her eyes back up to the Red Sister. That grin was so wide it practically glowed in the dark.

"Another question," Jaunda said.

Uh-oh ...

"If this goes well, what do you think of being our liaison?"

Irrwaer blinked. *Not what I was expecting.* "Isn't Tarra your liaison?"

Jaunda shrugged. "D'Shea doesn't like her that much. She thinks you're more interesting, like you see a bigger web like she does. She mentioned she might use the favor you'd owe us to ask Roshen to change our reps."

Ohhh, wouldn't that make Tarra so angry?

"I don't know what to think," she said without lying.

"Eh, alright. Still have to see how this goes with your bua, don't we?"

"Indeed."

They paused, listening for any sound behind the boulder.

Nothing.

Jaunda scratched her jaw. "Want some distraction while you wait?"

There it is.

Irrwaer huffed and shrugged. "Yes, Red Sister, I would."

"Great! Cunt or netherhole?"

"I don't care. You choose."

The Lead Sister chuckled. "Well, then. Guess I'll do both."

The muscular fighter followed through, starting with an unexpected series of pinching which took the place of the louder spankings. Regardless, Irrwaer's ass smarted, and her slit was naturally wet when her belly was pressed against standing rock by the larger female. Jaunda removed the minimum amount of clothing from them both to fit her phallus inside Irrwaer's cunt first.

It felt good. An instant, strong pleasure.

Without blending our auras ... ?

"*Ohhh!*" the Priestess moaned in utter surprise to feel her own arousal rise sharply within the first strokes.

"Yeah?" Jaunda breathed, sounding oddly hopeful.

"Mmm, yeah ..."

"Fuck ... yeah ..."

The Red Sister thrust harder, lightly biting her lobe; one callused hand reached around to hold one tit, the other pulled up her robes to go beneath, strong fingers pulling and squeezing on her folds. The Lead didn't switch holes until *after* Irrwaer had climaxed.

Alone.

Where had that sensitivity come from?

"Want to know my guess?" Jaunda whispered, her cock stretching out the Priestess's second, trusting hole.

"Mmmhuh?" Irrwaer's voice trembled. She held herself in place, still in shock and humming with afterglow as she was penetrated again, slow but constant.

"My guess. Why you just came like that ... I think your bua's having a good time. We should do the same."

They certainly gave it their best.

Irrwaer was sore but had climaxed thrice more, twice with Jaunda, by the time they'd each had enough. She also had the time to clean herself up with the water and cloths the Red Sister kept on her and nearly fell asleep waiting for her son to exit the cache.

"Mothherrr?"

She sucked in a startled breath. "Uh! I'm here!"

Irrwaer blinked at Vesram as he smiled with relief to see her. He was a mess, his mane was matted, and he smelled very strongly of sex, but there were only a couple shallow fingernail marks on his back which would be gone by the next cycle. He cuddled next to her, looking about to fall asleep as well. His stomach growled for food.

"Whew!" said one of the Red Sisters to her Lead. "*He* was pent up."

Jaunda laughed. "Don't doubt it. How was it?"

"Fun," said another. "Works hard, understands words, didn't try to cheat unless he wanted to be cheated. For a Sathoet, better than I expected."

"You can thank his Priestess." Jaunda winked at Irrwaer. "The only one I've heard of that healed her chosen demon-sire enough on the altar that he wasn't cumming from pain. Vesram's a pleasure-baby."

Her Sisters' eyes widened.

"Truly?"

"Wow."

"Well," said the third, hands on her hips, smiling at Irrwaer. "That is a first. Good work, Priestess."

"Huh. How might that shift the rituals if more Sathoet are like him?"

"I don't know, but I get why the Elder wants *her* as liaison."

Irrwaer finger-combed her tired son's sweaty mane, only able to smile and nod as they speculated above her head.

Too many know D'Shea's plans for this to turn out well.

Almost as many knew her son much better as well, and they weren't wary of him in the least. That was her own doing because she cared enough to want to teach him but couldn't do it herself.

Our preferences will only become harder to choose from now on.

Sometimes they had to change with the time.

Chapter 13

2979-2999 S.E. – The Palace-Sanctuary Complex

There were multiple warning signs over the next two decades, but none came close enough together to grasp any sense of urgency.

"Priestess Irrwaer, you've been requisitioned as a temporary resource for the Sisterhood. Your contact is Lead Qivni. You should get along. Qivni used to serve in the Sanctuary as well."

Roshen had at least been right about that.

"Priestess Irrwaer, we truly believe it is time that Vesram better know his brothers in the chamber. Even Kerse, as much time as he spends outside of it, knows the other Priestesses' Sons. You can't keep him apart from his own kind all his life."

Thank the Goddess the Red Sisters had given him some sparring lessons. He might have been half dead when she saw him again, but he'd held on without damaging a brother until she returned.

*"Priestess Irrwaer, we need you to tend the Royal Consorts while they're back at the Sanctuary resting before the next Worship Ball. You may **not** take your Sathoet on that floor, do you understand?"*

She had done her duty, but she hadn't been able to see past Ta'suil's beautiful mask. Juliran's son pretended not to recognize her the whole quad-span she was there.

What have they done to you, Sil?

"Priestess Irrwaer, you will take over liaison duties for Lelinahdara until she returns

from her pilgrimage. Elder D'Shea has requested to make this a permanent arrangement, but I would like to see how well you can protect the Sanctuary's secrets."

Oh, no.

Then, finally …

"You can't give in to her like that, High Priestess!" Tarra bellowed, pointing a finger at Irrwaer. "She is a *liability*, not a liaison! She's let the Red Sisters gang up on her own son, for Void's break! They know more about our ritual, the secrets of our power, than ever before and they want more to bring us down!"

"Is this true, Priestess?"

Ahhh, shit.

"OH, MY," WILSIRA BEGAN, FOLDING HER HANDS BEFORE HER. "HE'S IN QUITE rough shape, isn't he?"

Irrwaer's hands were shaking as she chose the first wound to stop the bleeding. Vesram rumbled in his throat, his eyelids fluttering but not opening.

"I could help you, healer. Kerse understands being different from the rest, and he's the eldest among them. Perhaps we could teach and learn from each other? It doesn't seem safe for our youngest in the chamber anymore."

Understatement of the century.

But Irrwaer had seen it coming after the last mass ritual.

They don't want our magic. We're being culled.

"Juliran has offered a place to stay while he heals," Irrwaer said.

"Oh? Has she? Odd. Are you sure you're safe with her? I understand she resents your lack of birthing scars."

Irrwaer felt light-headed. *The Conceiver knows.*

It didn't matter whether Juliran had told her under duress or not. She knew!

"I am very interested in how you managed this, young Priestess. Surely you should be higher than you are, to discover such a breakthrough."

The rest of you would never be able to do it.

Wilsira turned away and walked a few paces, pausing as if she expected her to follow. "Come with me, Irrwaer. I want to show you something."

"I need to help my son first, Conceiver. I'm sure you understand."

"Don't you want to know where D'Shea vanished to that one time?"

Goddess damn them all.

"I must concentrate," Irrwaer said through gritted teeth.

"Ah. Am I distracting?" The Conceiver chuckled. "Perhaps another time."

Finally, she left.

Moments later, Irrwaer's tears dropped onto Vesram's fevered skin as he whimpered trying to turn over on his side.

We need to get out, or they will kill us.

But she didn't have anywhere to go.

This must be what House D'Shea felt before they went extinct.

All but one surviving sorceress and her stolen son.

"Valsharess? Y-you summoned?"

"Come in, child."

Feeling very much in that role, Irrwaer still led Vesram out of the jump circle with as much poise as she could muster. They both kneeled upon the richly woven rug; her son was shivering. She set down the bloodstone that had brought her here, though she wasn't sure which floor of the Palace they were on.

Her Queen faced away from her, wiping down odd items and statues within a glass curio. Her blonde braid formed two coils upon the floor. When She turned around, Irrwaer studied how the braid curled around the hem of the purple gown like a furry reptile cuddling for warmth.

Meanwhile, she was sweating through the pits of her gown.

"We received your request to be reassigned," the Valsharess began. "It seems a bit too late, Priestess."

"I seek alternative service in Braqth's desires," Irrwaer murmured. "Like I did before with —"

Her throat nearly closed on the name.

" — D'Shea!"

The Queen tilted her head, seeming to notice the change. "Hm. And you went around your High Priestess to ask."

Irrwaer nodded. "I am a healer, my Queen, and it's become powerful. My son wasn't born like the others. The Sathoet want to kill him now like they want to kill the purebloods. He's safe nowhere but with me, Your Grace, but the other Priestesses only separate us at every turn. Every span, there's something else. And if he dies while I'm not there to protect him ..."

She choked on a sob. Vesram purred softly, touching her slipper with reverence.

"We understand this," said her Queen, Her tone softer now. "More than you can know."

Irrwaer tried to catch her breath, waiting in silence as the ancient Davrin pondered whatever drifted behind those translucent eyes.

"Do you want to know what vision We saw for you once?" She asked.

"Uh ... Yes, my Queen. I do."

"Alternative service," She said. "Serving Us on the Surface."

Irrwaer's eyes stuck at their widest. *The ... Surface?*

The place mentioned in sparse scrolls that hardly seemed real.

Beyond the Deepearth.

"We didn't know when this vision may occur," her Queen continued. "There were no landmarks around you. Perhaps that means We are to choose."

Irrwaer felt dizzy, weaving on her knees. Vesram gently took her shoulder when she might have toppled over.

"Well, Priestess? Shall We choose for you now?"

She was breathing far too fast.

Answer Her. Answer!

"M-may I bring my son to protect me? On the Surface."

The Valsharess sounded to be smiling. "Of course. We enjoy seeing this devotion."

"Wh ... what must we do, Your Grace?"

"You must find a tower far above Sivaraus," She answered with the greatest surety Irrwaer had ever heard. "The recent one built at the new crossroads."

"And … when we find this tower?"

"Prevent it from being claimed, Priestess. By any means. It must be empty for now."

Prevent it from …

"Claimed by who?"

Or what?

The Valsharess paused for much longer this time, and She didn't sound as sure in Her answer.

"It could be any among them," She said. "We only See them getting closer. It is not time."

Any suggestion she may have given for alternative service from the Sanctuary had not even scratched this option.

Leave Sivaraus. Leave the Deepearth?

Find a tower. A recent one.

She had to ask.

"Are we allowed to return home afterward, my Queen?"

The sense of the room grew heavy.

"Home?" The Valsharess paused. "Yes. If you can make it such distance."

Then what? What will we do when we return? Go back to the Sanctuary?

Irrwaer bit back against that flurry of doubt. "Are we to go alone, Your Grace?"

"No," She said. "We will send the Elder General to show you the way."

Just her?

Again, she bit her tongue.

The Elder General was only one rank below the Red Sister Prime. Maybe one General was worth any ten of the Sisterhood.

"You must move quickly," She declared. "We will summon her now."

Now?!

"Y-yes, my Queen."

The Valsharess paused with Her hand on the ornate strings of beads covering the door to another room. "Keep biting your tongue until We return."

"WHAT IN THE FUCK?" ELDER RAUSERY SAID MORE THAN ONCE BETWEEN THE JUMP circles leading them farther and farther out of the Great Cavern.

Each time, she glanced at Irrwaer and Vesram, arching one ruffled eyebrow. Both shrugged. Neither of them could talk about it.

The Elder Sister sighed, adjusting her pack. "You two are going to be so sore the first few days."

Days?

"We can heal," the Priestess replied.

"So I heard. Try to keep up and pay attention. You need to find water and food, and there are no servants out here to massage your feet."

The jab didn't hit as hard as the Red Sister probably thought it would.

"H-have you been to the Surface, Elder?" Irrwaer asked, testing her voice's reliability, which was greatly altered.

"Yeah. And save your breath for the climb. Plenty of time to talk when we rest."

Irrwaer fell silent, and once again the Elder muttered under her breath. *"I can't believe this."*

★So,★ RAUSERY BEGAN AS THEY SAT IN THE PITCH BLACK OF THE DEEPEARTH WILDERNESS. ★Short mission? Just to the Dwarven tower and back. We have enough rations to make it one way, and I can make up my mind whether to stake out with you or not.★

Irrwaer could nod her head, at least. She felt Vesram bump his muzzle into her back, looking for reassurance. She squeezed his thick forearm.

★What are you looking for?★

The Priestess shook her head, her mouth pressed shut. It wouldn't work correctly, anyway. Rausery sighed softly. She didn't seem surprised, nor did she sign what was slowly sinking in for Irrwaer.

That she and Vesram probably weren't coming back.

In asking to leave the Sanctuary before they killed us, we were sent into exile to die elsewhere.

Just with one last purpose, one she couldn't refuse.

At least She didn't take him away.

Maybe She didn't have that power.

CHAPTER 14

2999 S.E. – THE WESTERN LONELY ONES

THE SURFACE WAS A RUGGED PLACE, OVERWHELMING THEM WITH ITS SCENTS AND sounds. Warmth and chills came and went without cease; the air could never stand still. Thirst and hunger were far more intense despite their rarely being without food, and muscles and joints ached with the effort of navigating slopes covered in plants and slick mud.

Then came the rain, one of the most horrid experiences off the altar.

I'm so glad we've been blindfolded this whole time.

Rausery had explained that it would take her "weeks," many days and nights, to train her and her son to tolerate the Sun. Just with the glimpse they'd had already, stabbing white light into their eyes, the Priestess agreed they weren't up for that test of endurance. On account of it being easier to rest at night in the relative dark, even with the blazing moons floating in the sky, the Elder had to lead them blind through the aboveground mountains during the day.

Once, Vesram broke away from them with a snarl, launching toward something he heard. He brought back something small and bloody, crunching bones hungrily.

"Impressive," Rausery admitted. "A blind hunt. Share the next one with your mother, she could use the meat to keep healing you both."

"Yesss, Elderrr," he answered, dipping his head to her.

Irrwaer smiled with pride even though he couldn't see it; he could probably feel it. The Elder seemed even more impressed later when Vesram took her advice without a reminder.

"Eat," her son insisted, placing a bloody lump in her hand.

Irrwaer chuckled and took a big bite.

"Mothherrr?" Vesram rumbled.

"Yes. I feel it, too."

They had finally found the tower.

Although Irrwaer still wore her blindfold against the day, she didn't need the Elder General to tell her. She could *feel* it. She had been drawn to it for days now.

Magic flows like a river up here.

Ahead, the flow she'd been weaving through intersected with another.

The new crossroads. Just like She said.

Now, how to tell if anyone was there? If so, how would they scare them away so she could go home?

"Have to wait until night to see from this distance," Rausery pointed out.

Ever the practical one.

"You don't want to use the easy shelter?" Rausery asked after they'd kept watch on the massive, stone tower jutting out of the side of a mountain slope. There'd been no movement or light for most of the night.

It must stay empty.

Irrwaer shook her head, clutching herself.

"Be reasonable. There's water down there. It gets colder than you've seen up here. There will be a hearth to light a fire. Are you going to squat in a bush until you find what you're looking for?"

She's preparing to leave. Goddess, I'll be alone ...

132

Somehow, it didn't feel like Braqth's eye had followed her Priestess all the way out here.

Just those of her Grandson.

Rausery exhaled at her silence and shrugged. "Fine. Let's find a cave instead."

EVENTUALLY, THE ELDER GENERAL NEEDED TO LEAVE. SHE COULDN'T HELP IRRWAER in what she "sought," and the Priestess couldn't plan specifics with her. Instead, Rausery taught them some practical skills to stay in the vicinity for about a "month" or two.

"Head back before it gets too late," she warned. "There's a lot of food now, and it'll get hotter, but then it'll go the other way. Colder than you've ever been in your life, and no food. Just bare rocks and trees."

What kind of place is this?

Irrwaer nodded, despondent to watch her go. The General kept a lower and older vibe than Jaunda, but they were similarly grounded, respected non-mages who could smile and not talk about the senselessness of their goddess or their queen every cycle. Insane to think Irrwaer would miss this Red Sister more than anyone in the Sanctuary.

Vesram kept her warm through the next rainstorm to sweep through, and both suffered the harsher grey light to study the clouds blocking the Sun and dropping their water.

Madness. Unpredictable.

Yet they drank what the storm left behind, and so did the green things, and the flowers. Despite the fright from the winds and the cold, despite shaking her head at the disorder, the Priestess was beginning to see the cycles.

They slept through another day, one of many unmarked in any significant way, and woke to finally see a light shining within the tower.

They must have moved in while we were in Reverie! Fuck!

★We must discover who they are,★ she signed to her son, now that they could both see. ★Either chase them out or kill them.★

He chuffed, nodding. *Ready.*

They had crept partway there when Vesram paused and sniffed the air, turning his nose toward the right.

Irrwaer frowned. *Rabbit? Deer?*

The Sathoet shook his head, inhaling again. *Female. Two legs, long hair. Like you.*

Like me?

Not Rausery returning; he knew her scent, he would have said so.

He must be mistaken. There are no other Elves up here.

Fade yourself, she commanded. *Help me flank her.*

Vesram nodded and his nose led the way to an overhang with a good view of the valley below leading to the tower. He kept the scent and brought her to see a blonde female dressed in brown skins, with a bow and quiver resting against her pack. She leaned against a fallen tree, resting with her eyes closed. If she was an Elf, she had the ears but not the skin.

So pale.

Was she old? Did she lie out here because she was dying?

As they crept closer, Irrwaer saw the long legs, her tall, capable body, and her youthful face. If not for the golden hair and sickly pallor, this one could be beautiful.

Abruptly, the pale Elf woke. Panic entered her eyes.

Scare them away.

"Leave," Irrwaer growled. "What are you doing here anyway?"

The wild Elf sprang up, lithe and light as a deer, and sprinted up to the crest of the overhang. She nocked her bow and arrow with smooth practice, aiming at Irrwaer, her strange face displaying pure terror.

Incredible.

"Look at you!" the Priestess laughed in that surreal moment. "Are you a warrior, perchance? Do they call you the Pale Sisters?"

The blonde didn't understand her, this was obvious, but as soon as she drew the courage to draw her arm back, Irrwaer recognized when she bumped into Vesram camouflaged. Her Sathoet calmly reached over her shoulder, severed her bowstring, and pushed her over the edge without a second thought.

It was a natural response to anyone threatening his mother.

Breathless, Irrwaer rushed to seize a young tree and lean to look over the rise. The blonde may have tumbled to her death but slammed into another young tree and caught it in a strong grip of her own.

Damn.

Then the wild Elf filled her chest and started screaming pure babble at the top of her capacity. Irrwaer threw herself back in the grass, clutching her ears as the echo reverberated in her head.

What in the Abyss?!

She opened her eyes to see the archer was running full tilt down to the valley.

Toward the tower. Fuck!

She was *still* screaming when someone opened the door, revealing fire inside silhouetting two more bodies.

"Damn her," the Priestess hissed.

Why was she running? Did she know them?

She must, they are talking to her.

One was short and wide, but the other was tall and slim just like her.

They just let her inside …

Were pale-skinned Elves claiming the crossroads?

No. We can't have that.

"Mothherrr?" Vesram growled for further guidance.

"We need to wait and watch," she said, trying to remain calm and practical like Rausery. *Like Jaunda.* "There are at least three inside, now."

We must observe how to scare them away.

Or kill them.

"Let's retrieve our packs from the cave," she added. "We may need to move our den."

"Yesss."

They climbed back to the crest of the mountain and through the sloping meadow back to where they'd slept the last few weeks. They were nearly there when Vesram drew up and froze in place, his mane standing up before he crouched low in the long grass. Irrwaer followed him to the ground, giving him time to catch further scents as she listened to the wind.

Voices.

Low ones, roughly where their cave was.

Had they found their beds? Their supplies?

Shit.

These might be more from the tower. But then how had so many arrived at once, yet she and Vesram had heard nothing?

Then they smelled and heard the giant, snorting animals carrying two large sentients who clinked in their chains and armor. They were coming this way. The riders were absolutely *not* willowy female Elves.

★We must leave before they see us,★ she signed.

Vesram barely moved as branches and foliage crunched under heavy hooves, his concern and fret etched across his muzzle. He shook his head.

Too late to leave unseen. Fuck ...

She had a dagger with her and some spell components, but nothing assuring the instant death of an armored group. Vesram was the one who knew how to fight up close.

*This grows too big, too fast. We know nothing of these other races, and two of us aren't enough no matter what. We have no warriors! What are we **doing** here?*

She was here because she had asked mercy for her and her son from the Valsharess, who had *sent* them here vastly unprepared to serve a visionary purpose. Or as punishment.

Probably both.

Such was the way of Braqth.

Vesram had vanished from sight once again, and Irrwaer must be the bait. She sprang up and sprinted away from the cave, staying low and attempting to use the cover available. Unfortunately, the riders did not mistake her for a startled deer. Or if they did, they wanted the deer, too.

They shouted to each other and took chase.

Vesram was pacing her; she could feel him keeping close and see the parting swaths of tall grass. She chose a narrow path between two hills, less friendly for the large, clopping beasts. They charged through it, catching up to her on the other side.

As one large male leaned over, extending his hand toward her, his animal screamed at the large gashes that opened in its haunches and veered to the side, bucking him off.

Good bua! she thought, a sharp pain entering her side as she gasped for breath.

"Eyunkos!" called the other rider, choosing a split instant later to try for her rather than stop to aid his companion.

It had been a small chance he would, anyway.

Her son seized her, becoming fully visible, and pulled her away before the other male could grab her cloak. He used the tactic from the blonde Elf, filling his lungs, and shrieking, his mouth threateningly wide in the face of rider and beast. Irrwaer clutched her ears again as the mount reared up and kicked out at them.

"Shotan!" the warrior cried. *"Shotan shirir!"*

"Runnn!" her son said, launching with a firm grip on her arm. He was still able to move with much more agility and speed.

But held back because of me.

What skills did she have for this savage aboveground world?

The salt-white male forced control over his panicking ride before kicking the mount forward. When he caught up to them, he jumped from his saddle, landing upon her. His hands and body were more than heavy enough to drag her down.

She screamed as his armor bruised her legs, and Vesram whirled around and lunged, clamping his jaws directly on the warrior's face. Blood sprayed as fists and elbows struck her in the struggle. Irrwaer scrambled desperately away from the fighting males.

Once she regained her feet, she saw the other one running toward them on foot, without his mount.

"Shotan!" he cried, drawing a massive blade.

Oh, Goddess!

"Ai shuthrif cannin'ja!" she cried, casting the quickest, easiest cantrip she could think of.

His helm lit up bright enough for an altar room.

"Ai! Hai!" he cried, blindly clawing at the straps, dropping his sword.

The next moment, Vesram rushed by her and seized the thick neck in his mouth, growling, ripping, and tearing. Irrwaer looked behind her at the corpse of the first kill then retreated to make room as her demon-son fought for their lives.

The second warrior dropped, and Vesram sprayed blood from his mouth trying to breathe.

"Come," she called, beckoning to him. "Come with me!"

His strength was depleted, she could tell the moment he struggled to keep up with her in a sprint. She slowed as much as she dared, hoping for a second wind soon.

But they had no food. No water. And they couldn't leave the area around the tower yet.

Not yet.

If they tried to abandon their task, the warning pains were just beginning.

They found a place to hide and wait. In time, they heard their pursuers traipsing through the forest at night. There could be as many as ten, but the gait of two of them sounded odd.

Then her son smelled fresh blood.

There, Vesram signed.

Irrwaer couldn't believe her eyes. The two riders whom her Sathoet had just killed were … *Walking.*

Not alive, he confirmed. *Killed them. Still dead.*

Oh my Goddess …

Irrwaer turned her sight inward and could instantly see the mage among them controlling the corpses. A petite female with coloring opposite of the Davrin: white skin and black hair.

She's smaller than me.

The Priestess also recognized from their mannerisms that the remaining six larger, pale males were as protective of the death mage as Vesram was of his Priestess.

Except two dead men. They're just walking, carrying things.

Obeying, which still made eight of them.

Impossible.

There were too many for her son to fight, especially if the conflicts would be repeated over again.

★We should lead them to the tower,★ she signed as the idea came to her. ★Involve whoever was there for the other Elf. Maybe these death fighters are enemies.★

Vesram listened then nodded his silent agreement.

★Good. Let's go.★

They started to creep away and even earned enough distance from their hunters to breathe easier. But then, shortly before the tower would have been visible from the other direction, a strange feeling came over them. They stopped, bodies quivering, unable to take another step forward.

Irrwaer sank to the ground first, moaning in pain, and Vesram tried to shield her as he snarled in swelling agony. The Valsharess's voice came to her mind, bursting from recent memory.

"Prevent the tower from being claimed, Priestess. By any means."

Any means.

Including capture.

Sacrifice.

Their followers had heard their pain.

They were coming.

No.

"J-just one of us is enough," she forced out. "R-run to the tower, Vesram. You can make it. Maybe bring aid … ?"

Vesram hissed as she met his eyes; he could see she was truthful, even as neither could imagine him persuading the screaming blonde to aid him after pushing her down the mountain.

"No," he replied. "Ssstay."

What a time for him to grow disobedient.

Irrwaer looked over her shoulder, spotting the pale face of the small female first. She wasn't wearing armor. The Priestess looked back to her son, summoning as much command as she could bear.

"*Leave me*, Vesram! *Escape* before they kill you for killing theirs!"

He growled, his body jerking, his mane standing up as he stared at her eyes. "Cannnot ... leavve youu ... Mothherrr."

Irrwaer exhaled, noticing the pain lessening as their captors drew closer. She couldn't decide if she felt despair that he'd missed his chance or relief that she wouldn't face this alone.

It could be both.

Whether the tower would be empty or not, these travelers would never spot it from this direction. They might have if the Davrin and her Sathoet had been caught where they'd found the blonde Elf.

If that was all it took to serve her last purpose, so be it.

Irrwaer tucked closer to her son, embracing him as they waited for the strange warriors to surround them. Her bua held her tight, growling with defiance as the six warriors obeyed their orders from the small female without question.

They put away their weapons and brought out the chains.

Begin *Sister Seekers* with *No Demons But Us,* a polyamorous dark epic fantasy! at https://etaski.com/sister-seekers/

My name is Sirana, the Third Daughter of the Twelfth House.

My eldest sister broke her neck, and the Red Sisters suspect that I pushed her. If I take the blame, I am next on the sacrificial altar.

Dark Elves live for intrigue in our underground matriarchy. We bend the rules for the cunning and the bold. To survive, I must learn to play a dark and sensual game.

Court intrigue, demonic rituals, and mind-rending trials against deadly foes surround me, pervasive webs spun by our sadistic priesthood and the Queen's brutal enforcers.

Through it all, the Red Sisters delight in watching me. I must prove myself beneath their ravenous gazes or become the next meal for our goddess.

A.S. Etaski spins the first threads of an intense and epic tale with *No Demons But Us,* in which the trials of a young Davrin test her resolve to rise from the depths of fear and hatred tearing her down.

Sister Seekers is an adult epic fantasy with an ever-broadening scope. Found Family is a core theme throughout, and fans of "Dungeons and Dragons" will find familiar grounds. Perfect for fans of entwined plots, challenging themes, immersive worldbuilding, and elements of erotic horror. Sexuality and inner conflict play into character growth with nuance, intrigue, action, and magic.

Want to explore more the world of *Sister Seekers*? Do you enjoy maps and timelines, love glossaries, and reading extra details about the people, places, and objects in a story? Be sure to visit Etaski's website for more information and updates.

ACKNOWLEDGMENTS

Thank you so much, my friends and beta readers: Eris Adderly, Axelotl, Kangaroo, Dark Pulse, NecrosisBob, Pastor of Muppets, Leonard, and Ile Depak.

Much love and many thanks to my Hubs for believing in me.

Thank you, Doc Kangey, for your gifts of time, skills, and tutoring for the cornerstones of my career online. Check out our hard work and lore yet to come at Etaski.com & Miurag.Etaski.com

Finally, my enduring gratitude to my top patrons, who make paperbacks possible and support all my efforts to develop my writer's goals in every way:

Sir Cumference, Baelus, Jesse C., Does, John K., Julie S., Paul B., Carla H., Briana R., Josanna, RainbowNight, Lesley PLAY, Kalculyszero, NotSoWeird, Zenor , Kelly D., Lady Dia Meter, Raymond T., Lexanii, Zeroharas, Johnathon Matlock, Chris R., Christi L., and Roy Meyer, and in loving memory, Stacy Meyer.

ABOUT THE AUTHOR

Etaski has entertained herself with fantasy stories since the first day she sat on a school bus looking out the window. When hand-written letters were disappearing, she scribbled no less than five pages to be worth the postage. Her early stories were written by hand, and she had a writer's callus and three embarrassing novels before graduating high school.

She studied science, archaeology, history, and theater. Frank discussions of sexuality or death were rare growing up, so she wrote fantasies, theories, and observations within stories for deeper contemplation or just to be entertained.

History speaks little on sexuality, yet biology demonstrates how it sways basic choices. Drama reveals our strongest bonds but may fade to black at its most intimate. In the Sister Seekers, the sex and the story are inseparable, and their discoveries will change the journey of Miurag without cutting away.

Etaski's Website: etaski.com
Etaski's Series Lore: miurag.etaski.com
Etaski on Patreon: www.patreon.com/etaski
Etaski's Link-Tree: linktr.ee/etaski